Mor‹
The Lightness of

The Lightness of Water & Other Stories masterfully renders the lives of West Virginia characters displaced from the fragile land and culture of their deeply rooted ancestors. Fraught by the aftermath of coal mining and lumber companies, Rhonda Browning White's characters grapple with poisoned land, cancer, joblessness, and infertility. Despite the explosive circumstances, these stories are nuanced and finely crafted, infused with humor and humanity. This is a thrilling and highly satisfying debut collection by a craftswoman already at the height of her powers.
    —Susan Tekulve, author of *In the Garden of Stone*
        and *Second Shift*

The stories in Rhonda Browning White's excellent first collection are laid out in a perfectly balanced tension between the necessities and responsibilities of love–and ecological and personal catastrophe.
    —Meredith Sue Willis, author of *Their Houses*
        and *In Mountains of America*

One might describe the lives of the characters in this collection as hardscrabble, but that word "hardscrabble" would paint these characters and their stories with too broad and dismissive a brush, would suggest their lives are too far removed from ours. Rhonda Browning White's artistry and insight takes us so much deeper into the nuances of her characters' lives that we get to know them up close, recognize parts of ourselves within them, and see how much of their lives are our own— so much so we are moved, sometimes to tears, in the way great stories always move us.
    —Marlin Barton, author of *Pasture Art*

Rhonda Browning White's voice ranges from the Great Smokies of the early twentieth century to the contemporary language of OxyContin and mountaintop removal. Her memorable characters are a welcome addition to the Appalachian literary landscape.
    —Denise Giardina, author of *Fallam's Secret: A Novel*
        and *The Unquiet Earth: A Novel*

Rhonda White has given us memorable stories featuring extraordinary characters. The prose is assured and frequently lovely. She writes with a compassion and emotional precision that few short story authors can match.
    —Eliot Parker, author of *A Knife's Edge*

The Lightness of Water *&* Other Stories

THE LIGHTNESS OF WATER

& OTHER STORIES

Winner of the Press 53 Award for Short Fiction

RHONDA BROWNING WHITE

Press 53
Winston-Salem

Press 53, LLC
PO Box 30314
Winston-Salem, NC 27130

First Edition

Cover design by Claire V. Foxx

Cover image, "Holy River," copyright © 2009
by Dorit Jordan Dotan, liscensed through iStock

Library of Congress Control Number
2019942260

Printed on acid-free paper
ISBN 978-1-950413-07-2 (paperback)
ISBN 978-1-950413-08-9 (hardcover)

For Randy, who is everything.

The author is grateful to the fine literary journals in which these stories first appeared (some in slightly different form), as well as to their generous editors and discerning readers:

Bellevue Literary Review, "A Big Empty"

HeartWood Literary Magazine, "All Grown Up"

Hospital Drive, "Things Long Dead"

Prime Number Magazine, "Worth Fighting For"

Qu Literary Journal, "Bondservant"

Steel Toe Review, "Good Friends"

Contents

Bondservant

These mountains are killing me—killing all of us—though I know it's in self-defense. Getting away from here is all I can think about as I step off the bathroom scale, skim my jeans over my pelvic bones, take up the slack inch of denim with a safety pin. Another pound slid off me this week, even though I shoveled the last of an orange-glazed Bundt cake into my mouth yesterday. Missy's momma baked the cake for Paw, but my father-in-law wouldn't eat it, sent it home for Jasper and me to share. Paw won't eat much of anything these days. He went from mining to logging when coal dust sucked the air from his lungs, then from logging to sitting on the couch when his Crohn's disease turned to cancer and his body started dissolving. Like mine seems to be doing.

My ribs look more like a washboard now than four years ago in high school when they nicknamed me Bony Romie. Maybe I have Crohn's, too. It's wiping out half the mountain, what ones don't die of cancer or black lung. The GI doc in Bluefield told Paw he'd called the CDC down in Atlanta, told them they should start tracking it. Said it wasn't normal for Crohn's to nest in an area like it had in Stump Branch. Paw and the doctor think it has something to do with the coal mines—something they're pumping into the ground, or something they're pumping out—probably the same thing that's causing the grass to burn up and the fish to swell and lay on the riverbanks like wall-eyed shovel heads.

The smell of sweet cornbread baking wafts into the bedroom, and my mouth waters, but I don't care to eat. Food sometimes turns against me these days, causes a quick rush of nausea. It always passes, though. Paw told Jasper the same thing happened to him right before he was diagnosed.

I put away the pink Myrtle Beach 2012 T-shirt from our last vacation, pull down one of Jasper's bulky West Virginia Mountaineers sweatshirts instead. It'll hide my ribs and the little swollen paunch that's shown up low on my belly.

"Anybody home?" Jasper calls from the living room. Our trailer trembles when he slams the front door behind him, and I massage the dull ache building behind my temples.

I snatch the notice about the mountaintop-removal-mining protest from the dresser, shove it into the drawer before Jasper sees it. I hate the anti-MTR meetings and protests. The things they say about what's happening to the land and to us who live here scare me, give me nightmares even.

Yet I can't seem to stay away.

The woman who invited me to my first meeting in the back bay of Walker's Garage told me that what I didn't know could kill me. Since then, I haven't missed a meeting. I want to learn everything they're teaching, see firsthand the changes taking place in the people of Stump Branch.

I've seen a dozen locals become spies or environmental activists in a matter of weeks. Men and women I've known my whole life have turned into scientists who show us soil and water samples, toxicology reports, easily pronouncing six-syllable words and reading long lists of deadly chemicals—and one of those men never finished high school. Funny how staring at death makes people smarter.

I shove worry to the back of my mind, smooth my hair, and make myself smile, then head down our short hallway. "There's my man." I lean in to peck a kiss on Jasper's lips, the only part of him besides his eyeballs that isn't pitch black. "Did the night shift treat you all right?"

Jasper nods, sets his lunch bucket on the vinyl runner by the door, slides out of his coal-stained twill coat. "I smell corn bread." His blue eyes light like propane flames, their brightness intensified by the mask of coal dirt surrounding them.

"Can't have brown beans without it," I say.

"Mmm, lady! I'd marry you again, if you weren't already mine."

I swat at him. "Get cleaned up. Corn bread'll be done in a jiffy." I turn off the warming flame beneath the pan and spoon potatoes fried with onions into a blue-speckled bowl. "Might want to bring in your work boots off the porch, set them in the tub. We're supposed to get a skiff of snow later this morning."

"Too early for snow. I ain't ready for it, yet." From the bathroom down the hall, Jasper's voice echoes as if he is still deep inside the mine. "You check on Daddy after work yesterday?"

"I did." I add a thick pat of golden butter to the fried potatoes, the same thing I made for my father-in-law yesterday, and I think of the man's yellowing, wary eyes. Paw—I've always called him Paw instead of Daddy, out of respect for my own daddy who died when I was twelve—Paw's sliding downhill fast. It isn't just his sickness, either. His mind ain't acting right. He's not himself, and I worry he's up to something. A no-good sort of something.

A long pause settles between us before Jasper asks the heavy question I know will follow. "He send any more Oxy home with you?"

"On the bedroom dresser." I set the table, stand by the kitchen window and watch the morning sunrise illuminate the miles of flat, beige scab that used to be a cloud-grazing piney mountain. I unclench my teeth and work my aching jaw.

Ten minutes later when Jasper pads out of the bathroom bare-chested, barefoot and smelling of soap, I slide the pone of steaming corn bread onto the table. "Want milk for dunking?"

"Heck yeah." He flashes his white smile, and just like that, my icy mood melts.

Jasper picks up a slab of corn bread, slathers it with butter, takes a big bite, and talks around it. "How many pills did he send this time?"

I look out the window again, listen to the harsh wind whistle past the windowpane. No deep folds of mountain, no heavy forest out there anymore to hedge us in, protect us. "Didn't count 'em." I break off a piece of corn bread, crumble it between my fingers, watch the grains sprinkle onto the plate. "Felt like too many." I dust my hands together and take a long swig of milk to wash away the bitterness on my tongue.

"You'll wish you had more, the day comes you ever need to sell 'em."

I thump down my glass hard enough to make my fork jump. "Dammit, Jasper, you been dying since the day you walked into that mine. I'm tired of you always planning for the day you don't come home." I stand, rake my food into the garbage can, and run scalding water over the plate.

"Don't be like that," Jasper says. "Sit down, honey. Eat."

"Not in the mood for cornbread," I say.

"Want me to make you a sandwich? Peanut butter is my specialty."

"I'm not hungry." I dry the plate, and I startle when Jasper breathes into my hair, slides his arms around me, pulls me back against his chest. I rest there, let his warmth seep into me. "We talked about this when I started working for Prospect. You know the chances I got of coming home in a box."

I know. Oh, yes, I know. Roof bolting is about the most dangerous job an underground miner can do. It also pays the most.

Jasper nuzzles my neck and whispers in my ear as his hands move lower on my stomach. "Babies cost money, and if we want a little Grodin some day, I need to stick around there a while."

I squeeze his hands, slide them a bit higher. How I ache for a baby in the hollow of my belly, pray day and night for a child. A selfish prayer, premature, but one that, if God will answer, might help Jasper see the sense in leaving this place. Stump Branch might cradle Grodin family land, but it's no longer the place for Jasper and me to start our family. The land is sick, the people are sick, and now I'm feeling sickly, too.

I turn around in Jasper's arms, look up into his once-smooth face, now lined and creased a decade beyond its twenty-two years. "You promised you'd quit in five years."

He nods, and a trickle of water sluices from a light-brown curl, skims his neck, and slides onto his chest. "Still got part of one to go."

"We could get out now, Jasper, go to North Carolina. Plenty of textile jobs down there. Construction jobs."

"You ain't got no reason to worry about me spending a lifetime underground. I can't stick around there no longer than six or seven years, anyhow."

"Six or seven years! You mean you'd stay longer?"

"We're less than a year from tearing into the last big coal seam on the property. After that, no more underground mining. Prospect's doing everything aboveground. MTR mining all the way. I'm the last of a dying breed, baby." He grins.

"Jasper, nobody says you got to stick out the full five you'd promised. Besides, Stinson didn't keep his word, neither. You still ain't got no medical card. You have to beg for a day off and lie to take one."

He tilts his head, touches his lips to mine, and electricity snaps between us. I flatten my hands on his chest, push him away. "Finish eating, and get some sleep. I have to run into town. I'll check on Paw again while I'm out. I believe he's supposed to see the doc again tomorrow. He thinks he can drive, but I want to make sure."

Jasper eases onto the straight-backed chair awkwardly, gingerly, like an old man.

"Your back bothering you again?" I ask.

"Not too bad. Big slab of roof fell today." He lifts his palms heavenward. "Had my hands up just so, caught the edge and shoved it to the side before it crushed Jimbo. I might have twisted wrong." He rolls a shoulder, arches, then digs his spoon into the beans. "Say Paw's going again tomorrow? Didn't he just go a few days ago for that scope?"

I take a deep breath, let it out slowly, quietly. "They go more often when it gets to end-stage." I watch him carefully, but he won't look at me. "The doctor called and said the big polyp he took out last week showed more cancer. Said Paw needs to have another ten or twelve inches cut out of there, but your daddy won't hear of it. Said no more knife."

"No more knife," Jasper echoes, pushing food around his plate.

"I'm sorry, Jasper. I know you hate talking about these things."

"So . . . what's Daddy gonna do?"

I watch my husband for a moment. He wouldn't want

me to candy-coat the truth. "He told the doc to double up on his pills if he would, but no more cutting."

Jasper chews slowly, puts down his spoon and looks up at me.

I hold up my hand, stop him before he can speak. "He needs them pills himself, Jasper. You know he's got to be hurting."

"Ain't like I'm taking anything he ain't offering. His idea to skim off the bottles, not mine." He breaks off another wedge of corn bread, dunks it into the milk. "He don't take half of what they prescribe for him, anyhow. Said if he took Oxy at the rate the doctor pushed it on him, he'd O.D. in an hour."

I turn away before I wipe my eyes, so Jasper won't see.

"Besides," he says, "I told him he ever needs them back, I got them right here, and I'll come running. Told him I'd never sell them, anyhow. They're yours for when—"

"For when you die! Hell yes, I know that!" My eyes feel like they're on fire, and I look toward the door. I want to be away from this room, from this house, from this place.

Jasper shrugs, bites off the sopping corn bread, swallows with hardly a chew. "It's the only life insurance policy we got."

I blink hard, his words stinging me like a slap to the face. I yank Jasper's good hunting jacket from the coat tree by the door, shove my arms into it, and push the cuffs over my wrists. "I'll try to be back before you leave," I say.

Then Jasper's words circle through my head again. *Caught the edge and shoved it to the side before it crushed Jimbo.* My Lord.

I speak a bit softer. "You pulling a twelve again? What time you go in?" He doesn't answer, and when I turn, Jasper's eyes catch me, hold me in the way that hurts my heart.

"Baby, come here." He holds out an arm, and before I know it, I'm wrapped up inside him, he's wrapped inside me.

*

With the groceries bought, the electric bill dropped off, and what's left of Jasper's check deposited, I head back up the mountain toward the Grodin homeplace, almost wishing it wasn't my day off work. Not that I like calling sick folk who can't afford their medical bills to remind them a turnover to collections is looming, but it sure beats watching Paw die.

The Jeep rocks like a boat among waves as I try to straddle the ruts and climb the ridge toward Paw's place. I peer into the skeletal tree line as the afternoon sun begins to sink, but I find no colorful fall leaves, no late green shoots, no encouragement that spring will follow winter, will ever come again to Stump Branch.

As I near the top, I slow and steer the Jeep to hug the inside of the narrow road, my stomach fisting in anticipation of meeting one of the monstrous coal trucks that race up and down the ridge all hours of the day and night. Since Prospect opened the mine in '98, each year someone has died either in a head-on collision or from being run over the steep embankment by a coal truck. Prospect always pays the fines, but they've never lost a court case, and no family has ever received a settlement for loss of life. My fingers ache from gripping the wheel too tight, and I flex them, telling myself that maybe tonight I will paint my nails for Jasper, telling myself anything to get dying off my mind.

I let out a pent-up breath when I round the blind turn without meeting a coal truck. A jarring blast from the mine a mile and a half away further stretches my nerves, and I grit my teeth as loose dirt and rubble tumble from the steep shale bank above onto the Jeep's roof and hood. You can't ever have anything nice around here.

Topping the knoll, I gaze out the passenger window at the bleak desolation below. Another big gray slurry pond—

nearly the size of a lake—burbles and pops where once a field of Queen Anne's lace, wild strawberries, and morning glories ambled over the ground. Nearly seven years have passed since they dug the pond, and not a weed nor blade of grass grows within a hundred yards of it. Poison slop. Full of arsenic, copper, selenium, and other chemicals I can't yet pronounce but have heard named at the anti-MTR coalition meetings. I study the pie charts they show us, and I always pay special attention to the one depicting water quality, where the chemicals cover all but a blue sliver of the pie. A pond can't hold in that kind of misery for long. Nothing can.

After the turn-off toward Paw's place, the Jeep travels smoother road along the man's well-tended drive. I pull alongside his mailbox, reach out the window and retrieve a handful of doctor bills, insurance notices, and the same anti-MTR flyer that was in my mailbox yesterday. Paw hasn't been outside since my last visit.

The house hasn't changed much since the first time Jasper brought me home to meet his folks six years ago, right after he'd gotten his driver's license. The white clapboards don't look as proud now that coal dust stains the crevices, and though Paw usually keeps up with the ditch lilies Momma Grodin planted the year before she died, he hasn't cut them back this fall, and they lay like heaps of wilted broomstraw along the edge of the porch.

Paw doesn't come to the door as he usually does when I drive up, so I jump out of the Jeep and mount the steps two at a time. He could be in the bathroom, I tell myself, trying to banish bad thoughts.

I knock at the door, three quick raps. "Paw?" I open the door without waiting, knowing my father-in-law's front door has never been locked. As easy to lock the boogeyman in as out, he says. May as well let him come and go as he pleases.

"Paw?" A rush of heat wraps around me, nearly takes my breath, and I cross the wooden floor and check the thermostat. Eighty-five. "Where are you, Paw?"

"Be out in a minute." His voice sounds strangled, and he rattles a wet cough.

Bathroom. I drop the mail on the coffee table, shed Jasper's coat and lower the thermostat to seventy-three. "It's hotter than Hades in here, Paw. You got the chills or something?"

The toilet flushes, followed by running water at the sink, then Paw emerges. "I've been a little chilly, yeah."

I suck in a breath. His face has grayed overnight, and his eyes have sunk so deeply into their orbits that he looks like the plastic Halloween skull I put on our front porch last week. He offers a strained smile and walks cautiously down the center of the wide hallway, as if barefoot on broken glass.

I rush to his side. "Paw, my Lord, why didn't you call me?" Once a foot taller than me, Paw now walks with a stoop, and he levels his hollow gaze with my stare. "You look a mess," I say. It's an understatement.

Paw grins around his grimace, and his watery eyes make me want to cry.

"Ain't nothing you can do for me, doll baby," he says. "If they was, I'd tell you." He pecks a hot, dry kiss on my cheek. "'Sides, I'm getting along just fine for an old feller."

When I slide an arm around Paw's back, his spine presses against my arm through my sweatshirt. He feels so light I think I could carry him on my hip, like a baby. "Let's rest a bit, why don't we?" I say. He leans on me as I lead him to his recliner and help him sit. "Can I get you anything? Drink of water? Coffee?"

He lifts a bent finger and points toward the kitchen. "Just put on a pot about six hours ago. Ought to be stout by now. Black. No sugar, sugar." He grins at his joke, but his lips are thin and tight, and another cough bubbles in his throat.

"Want me to take you to the hospital, Paw?"

"No. Next time I come out of this holler, it'll be in a box."

I can't stifle a groan. "Great. Now you and Jasper are both talking that foolishness." I fill two mugs, add a spoonful of powdered creamer to mine, carry them into the living room.

"What's got Jasper dying today?" Paw asks.

"Slab of roof fell while he was bolting. I swear, Paw, between worrying about him and you, and the blasting that goes on all hours of the day and night, I ain't had a solid night of sleep in a month."

Paw's gaze settles on the fluorescent pink flyer that came in the mail. "Reach me that thing."

I curse myself for not throwing it in the trash before he saw it. "Aw, you know it's another piece of propaganda. They're right, of course, those protesters. But it ain't doing no good, and it only serves to stir up trouble and hurt feelings."

He grunts, and I don't know if he's agreeing or dis-agreeing. I push to find out. "Need to take their fight to Charleston, or maybe Washington. Only making people feel bad who have to earn a living in that mine. Ain't like the men's got a choice."

"Everybody's got a choice." He sips the steaming brew, sets his mug on the side table. "They got a right to protest, and what they're saying is the truth, Romie. Prospect Mining is killing all of us, what ones are working in the mines, and what ones ain't." He stares off for a moment, then speaks softly to the air. "I've had enough of it."

He turns and fixes me with a serious stare. "Jasper don't know you go to them anti-MTR meetings, does he?"

His question catches me off guard, and I wonder how he knows, who might have told him. "No, sir. I've only been to a couple. I just wanted to see what they were about."

"You ought to go to all of 'em. Don't miss nary a one."
He points again at the flyer.

I hand the stack of mail to Paw, taking care to shuffle
the flyer to the bottom. His words sound foreign to me.
He's long supported the miners, worked the mines himself
in the years when men only went underground, gouged
deep to get the coal instead of decapitating mountains.
Used to say underground mining might not be the best
way to treat Mother Nature, but it sure beat chopping off
her head like Prospect has started doing now.

Paw's glistening eyes rove the hot-pink page, then he
lays the flyer on the table, sips again from his coffee mug.
"They're going about it all wrong." He stares silently at
the dark TV for a full minute. Then he turns to me. "Say
you'll help me, if I need it?"

I wipe the dampness from my forehead, wish I'd worn
my T-shirt instead of Jasper's sweatshirt. "Think you
ought to go to the hospital, after all? Let's get you a bag
together." I stand and head toward my father-in-law's
bedroom.

"Sit down. I told you I ain't going to no hospital." He
stares at me in a hard way that tells me not to argue. "I
want your word that you'll carry out my last wishes."

My throat clogs. I try to think of a joke, something
funny to lighten his mood, but the words won't come.
Momma Grodin's old cuckoo clock sounds from the
kitchen, as if telling me it's time to listen, time to do what
Paw wants me to do while time is left. "Of course I will,
Paw," I whisper. "You know that."

He points. "Reach me that Bible."

I lift the worn, oxblood Bible from its place on the center
of the coffee table, offer it to Paw.

He puts on his bifocals with trembling hands, then opens
the leather-bound text to the last pages. "Let me read you
something."

I try not to look surprised, but it's hard. I know Paw reads the Bible, believes in the Lord above, but he's never preached to anyone, always says a man must find God on his own terms, and that he can find Him anywhere.

"The Book of Revelation," Paw says, "eleventh chapter, verse eighteen . . . 'The nations were angry, and your wrath came, as did the time for the dead to be judged, and to give your bondservants the prophets their reward, as well as to the saints, and those who fear your name, to the small and the great; and to destroy those who destroy the earth.'" A wet cough gurgles its way out of Paw's chest, and he snatches a tissue from the side table, closes his Bible.

He composes himself, and when he looks at me, his eyes are puddled. "You get that, Romie? 'To destroy those who destroy the earth.'"

I start to nod, but shake my head. "I get it, Paw. I think."

"I want to be a bondservant."

Dread slops over me like smothering slurry, and I ache to have Jasper here to hold my hand, to pull me to fresh air. "I don't . . . what are you saying?"

Paw dabs at a watering eye with the tissue, points toward the coat closet by the front door. "You done give me your word. Now look in there. On the floor."

I stand, and my feet feel heavy, like they're stuck to the carpet. "What do you mean? About being a bondservant? How does that work?"

He points again toward the coat closet, but doesn't speak.

I think he must have taken some OxyContin that's made him loopy, and that's a good thing. He surely needs it. I open the dark wooden closet door and stare at the strange thing on the floor. I step closer, realize it's a hunting vest that stands rigid, rust-colored sticks of dynamite holding it erect. My knees want to buckle. "Paw." The word comes out on a half-breath.

"Destroy those who destroy the earth."

I kneel in front of the closet. "No."

"What time's Jasper go in tonight? Five?"

"No, Paw."

"Look at me, Romie."

I turn my head a bit, but my stare won't leave the hunting vest.

"All I need is for you to drive me up there."

"People will die, Paw! You will die. We have friends at that mine. *Jasper* could be in that mine!" I finally turn to meet his gaze.

His smile comes easier now; his face is peaceful. "I'm already dead, doll baby. Only a matter of timing."

It's a struggle, but I manage to hold back a sob.

"Jasper will be going in soon, won't he? I could go into the mine this evening at shift change, during their meeting," he says. "They always meet in that old office trailer near the entrance. Either way, won't be a soul underground, 'cept me." He holds out his palms like Jesus on the cross. "You take me up there, go interrupt the meeting to see Jasper, tell him loud and clear something's wrong with me."

I shake my head to clear the cobwebs—can he really be saying these things?

"Say it loud, so the others will hear. Tell them you came straightaway to get help . . . phone's out, so you couldn't call for an ambulance."

Paw lets his hand fall between his recliner and the end table, and when he lifts it again, he holds up the phone line he's cut, so I can see its frayed edges. He gives me a white-lipped grin. "I'll mosey down past the equipment bays while you've got their attention. You and Jasper will be off the ridge before I let her blow. The ones atop the ground'll shudder and shake, but they won't be hurt none."

He wipes his mouth with the back of his hand. "The shafts will collapse . . . mining equipment will blow all to pieces. It'll cost more to wade through the EPA and OSHA paperwork and replace all that equipment than it will to shut her down. They'll clear out of here." Fresh pink blooms on his pasty cheeks.

My racing heartbeat slows, and I chew on a fingernail. It can't be that easy, can it? Jasper won't have a job, a place to work. If he's unemployed, we'll have to leave the state for work, won't we? Get out of here. Have a baby in a place where the water isn't chemical soup.

"It's my dying wish." Another cough breaks from his chest, and this time red dots spot the tissue.

I lurch toward Paw, wrap him in my arms.

"All you need to do is give me a ride," he whispers.

After a moment, he pushes me away from him, holds me at arm's length. "They done killed more'n five hunnerd mountains in this state and four times that in people. Somebody's got to show them we ain't gonna take it no more." He shakes his head. "They poisoned me." He pokes a finger at my stomach. "And they're poisoning you. You, and Jasper, and everybody else in Stump Branch."

I look down at the concave void just below my ribs, and I imagine a mound there in its place, a swollen womb full of Jasper's child. I dry my wet face on my sleeve. "Don't you want to talk to Jasper about this first?"

Paw shakes his head, and tears slip out again. "That'd hurt worse—hurt me and him both." He looks away, wipes his sunken cheeks. "It's better this way, he don't know." He motions toward the small table by the front door with a shaky hand. "There's two more stock bottles of OxyContin sittin' there, both plumb full. Ought to be enough to buy a new start in Carolina."

I follow the direction his fingertip points, look at the big, white, square bottles. Has to be more than a hundred pills in each, a dollar a milligram. Thousands of dollars pressed into little blue tablets.

Paw pats my hand, rubs away the dampness on my cheek with his thumb. "I done laid out my UMWA life policy on the bed, ready for you and Jasper to take to the lawyer. Ain't much, but it'll help. There won't be no funeral, nothing left to bury."

I squeeze his hand. "I know you think you've thought this through, but them mine owners won't shut down. They'll just lop off another mountain on down the road. Jasper's already said that's their next plan. And that life insurance policy—it won't pay for suicide."

Paw waves his hands, and his voice comes out in agitated wheezes. "I'm sick, Romie. They'll say Oxy stunned me . . . old man wasn't thinking right. He got confused . . . went to the mines . . . thought he still worked there." He swallows against the gurgle in his throat. "That much dynamite . . . all the gas that builds up around there . . . they'll never even know I blew the place. What's left of that hollowed-out mountain . . . it will be gone. Insurance will pay, you bet. It's the United Mine Workers Union."

"They'll fight it. You know they'll fight it. Insurance companies don't care about us."

Paw's bushy eyebrows lift, and again I'm struck by how gaunt his face has become.

"Prospect'll make 'em pay. You think they want word to get out? That one of their own blowed up a mine . . . on purpose? That miners are turning against the mines?" He clears his throat. "No, they'll want to cover it up . . . quick as they can . . . money's the best way to do that. They think money'll shut up anybody."

I grind my teeth, shake my head. "Paw, this is your sickness talking. I'm taking you to the doctor." I stand and offer him my hand, but he waves it away. Instead, his gnarled hands grip the armrests, and he thrusts himself forward, upright.

"Get my jacket."

I take a deep breath. *Finally, he's thinking right.* I return to the closet by the door and pull out Paw's flannel coat, averting my eyes from the hunting jacket.

Hunched forward, Paw eases toward the door. "Not that one." He points at the hunting vest. "That one."

"Humor me, Paw. Put this on." I hold open the flannel coat, guide Paw's long arms into the sleeves.

"Humor *me*, now." He jerks his head toward the open closet. "Get it."

It's not a bad idea to get the dangerous thing out of the house. I can set it over the hill and send Jasper to take it apart later. I pick up the heavy vest, surprised that it takes both hands to lift it. I look toward Paw, but he's headed out the door, trusting me to do as he said. I slide the vest onto one arm, and then I see the two medicine bottles. I look toward the ceiling. Would it do any good to pray? I heft the vest against my hip, and my hand trembles when I pick up the large bottles and slip them into Jasper's deep coat pocket. I hurry out the door to steady Paw as he ambles down the porch steps.

When we reach the Jeep, I set the hunting vest on the ground, help Paw climb inside, and start to close the door.

He grabs my arm and tilts his head toward the vest. "I'll take that."

"Bumpy as this road is, we'll blow to Kingdom Come before we get off the mountain."

"Who's the master blaster here? I've hauled dynamite around most of my life. It won't blow unless somebody blows it." He reaches out his hands, and his voice is stern. "I said I'll take that."

I peer into the bone-dry woods on the other side of the driveway. I've never disrespected my father-in-law. Never spoken a harsh word to him. He and Jasper's mother treated me like their own child from the first time I stepped into their home.

My shoulders sag as I lift the awkward vest, ignoring Paw's outstretched hands, and place it in the floorboard at his feet. I close the door, walk around the Jeep, and slide behind the wheel.

The pills clatter inside the bottles in my pocket, and Paw looks at me and smiles. "Good girl," he says, his voice hoarse. "I hate it's come to this. Shame you two got to sell them pills to make a life, but the Good Lord always provides, don't He?" He clears his throat, sinks backward into the seat and sighs. "I'm looking forward to meeting Him."

I press my lips together to keep from cursing. "Hope you know we're going to the hospital."

I glance toward Paw, but he won't look at me, keeps his gaze on the homeplace as I head down the graveled drive.

"Last time I'll be seeing this place."

"Don't say that."

"Romie, I won't last another day or two. I don't want to die in no hospital."

"You can stay with Jasper and me." I reach the end of the drive, brake, and the digital clock on the dashboard reads 4:44. The numbers seem like a message; one I can't decipher. I turn to look at Paw. "I'll take care of you."

"No pride in that. I'm a strong enough man. Still got one more job to do."

I look out across the rutted road, once smooth blacktop, now fractured into a million pieces by the overburdened trucks hauling out tons of mountain soul. Beyond that, what was once the rising mountain where I picked blackberries, chewed teaberry leaves, and made love to Jasper among blooming dogwoods is now low-lying, scarred craters—sterile, desolate, and barren. No place to live. No place to birth a baby. Only a place for dying. A place for destroying those who destroy this good earth.

I take Paw's hand in mine, kiss it, let him go. I hold tightly to the wheel, turn onto the road and drive toward the mine.

"I love you like a daughter, Romie. You're a real good girl. Thank you for doing this."

"I ain't doing nothing but taking you to see Jasper, let him talk some sense into your head. Lord knows I can't."

Paw's fist slams the dashboard, and I flinch.

"I told you I don't want Jasper in on this." Red-tinted saliva flies from his lip, and he wipes his mouth on the back of his hand, glares out the window.

"When you brought me in, you brought Jasper in." Another blast at the mine causes the Jeep to vibrate, and I grip the wheel tighter, shoot a sideways glance at the hunting vest standing in the floorboard between Paw's feet. "You sure that thing won't blow?"

"Got to light the fuse, first." Paw pulls an old Zippo lighter from his pocket, flips open the metal lid.

"For God's sake, Paw! Put that thing away."

Paw shoves the lighter into his coat pocket, speaks with a soft voice full of hurt. "I would never lay harm to you. You ought to know that."

I reach the entrance, drive past the Prospect Mining sign. I want to throw up, rid my stomach of the nerves writhing like snakes inside it.

Paw touches my arm. "Stop here, and let me out." His voice warbles, and he clears his throat. "By the time you get to the trailer, I'll be at the equipment bay entrance. You get Jasper, and y'all get off this mountain. I figure it'll take me a good fifteen minutes to get to her first belly. That's where I'll . . . you know . . . let her blow."

I set my jaw, press the gas pedal, and cut the wheel, slinging red-dog gravel and coal dirt in an arc across the wide parking area as I drive toward the office trailer. "I'll do no such thing. I'm going to get Jasper, all right, but only so's he can straighten you out. You're going to sit right here while I do it, you hear me?" I turn off the Jeep and snatch the keys from the ignition. "If you can look your son in the eye and convince him to go along with this fool idea of yours, I'll stand with you on it. But I won't let you put this burden on my shoulders to carry alone."

I step out, turn, and glare at Paw. "You staying put?"

I want him to say *no*. Want him to sling that heavy vest onto his shoulder, march like the soldier he'd once been into that mine, defend his family, defend this land, even at the cost of what few days he's got left. My face grows hot, fired by coals of shame smoldering inside me.

Paw's lower lip thrusts outward, and he reaches into the floorboard, tries to lift the heavy vest onto his lap.

I hold my breath.

Paw grunts and strains. "Help me put this thing on."

I look skyward, blinking hard and fast. Overhead, a lone red-shouldered hawk screeches, searches the gray mine in lonesome circles, moves on. I look again at my father-in-law, wonder if maybe I should do this God-awful thing that he asks of me. "Paw?"

Another rattling cough shakes his body. He lets the vest fall against the floor, leans back to catch his breath. He presses his steel-blue lips together, stares straight ahead, won't look at me.

Ahead of us sits the trailer, and I know Jasper's in there, know this is the place where he spends his nights and part of his days making a living for us, making a life for us, and in a way I can't pretend to understand, he likes mining coal. How can I take that away from him?

Paw drops his head, stares at hands curled like dead leaves in his lap. He sniffs and turns to me, lets out a long, jagged breath. "Useless," he whispers.

I climb back into the Jeep, pull out a handful of fast-food napkins from the console, and offer them to Paw. When he won't take them, I put all but one in his lap and dab the blood-tinged spittle from the corner of his mouth.

"This ain't the way you want to go out of this world, Paw. You're too good for that kind of destruction."

He looks out the window, surveying the wasted mountain. "I'm a foolish old man." His chin quivers.

"No. No, you're not."

A wet cough rattles Paw's body, and I turn my face away. "What say we go, before the men come out of that trailer?"

He picks up a napkin with a trembling hand and swabs his damp face as I start the Jeep and turn it around.

I wipe my eyes as I drive past the Prospect Mining sign.

Paw stares out the window toward the eight-mile fissure where once stood a mountain. He reaches over, pats my hand where it grips the gearshift. He lets out a ragged sigh, turns his ashen face toward mine. "You done the right thing."

I try to smile at him, but can't. "It ought to feel like it then, oughtn't it?" I glance at the rust-colored dynamite, push away second thoughts, and drive down the broken road toward home.

Things Long Dead

I'm hard pressed to tell you how I feel when I stroke my beard and look up from my barstool in Roadhouse 44, and I catch Lieutenant Finnegan's reflection in the sooty mirror behind the liquor shelves. I ain't sure if the prickle on my scalp is one of foretelling, like when time slides around and I know things ahead of God's time for them to happen, or if it's anger from knowing I've finally caught up with the lying sack of shit. I haven't set eyes on him since 'Nam. The prickle might even be pleasure I'm feeling; the satisfaction of seeing a living piece of my death-filled past. I watch him a good five or six minutes before he meets my glare in the reflection and leans over the bar to gawk down its length at me. We've aged, but I know he recognizes the star-shaped scar that covers the side of my head, the place where hair hasn't grown since the seventies. I lift my beer bottle, but it ain't a toast. More like fair warning, and I feel good about giving him that. It's more than he ever gave me.

He slides off his stool and swaggers toward me with that same arrogant saunter that used to irritate me worse than jungle rot. Nowadays, he's wearing black leather chaps instead of fatigues, and his thighs creak against each other when he draws near. I turn to face him.

Front Toward Enemy. I see the words in my mind today as clearly as I saw them the day they sent me sailing through the air.

"Fuzz!" he says, clapping me on the shoulder.

My jaw tightens, but I push out a smile anyway. "Lieutenant," I say, and I accept his handshake.

His face colors the way it always did when his empty head clouded. "You don't have to call me that now, Fuzz. Vietnam is way behind us. They call me Crankshaft these days." He pats himself on the back—physically, this time—and his face stains a shade deeper. "Never mind. Vest is in my saddlebag." He hooks a thumb toward the hand-lettered sign hanging over the bar. "No colors allowed in here."

Like I didn't know that, couldn't read. I'd shed my Thunder Hogs vest when I parked my bike out front, laid it atop the pink baby blanket in my saddlebag. See, the V.A. thought working with newborns would help me re-find my appreciation for life, so I volunteered at the local hospital—they need people to hold the preemies and sick babies, say it helps them thrive. I'd held "Walker, Baby Girl" off and on for weeks, and she was a fighter, a real soldier. Her first day out of NICU, she snuggled against my chest and quit breathing. I didn't know I was screaming until the charge nurse pulled her out of my arms, let her blanket fall to the floor. They worked and worked on her, but she never breathed again. I picked up her blanket, walked out of the hospital, and I never went back. Even when you hide among brand-new life, death will find you.

And now it's found Lieutenant Finnegan.

A slimy-looking grin slides across the lieutenant's face as he eyes my Harley T-shirt. "You ride?"

I nod, pull a swig from my beer, swallow, and run my

tongue over my teeth, feeling their hardness. I want to bite him. Tear meat from his bones.

"Ain't seen you in here before. You down on vacation?"

"Moved here a few months ago."

"That so?" His red-dog eyebrows lift. "What brought you to New Smyrna?"

"Came for Bike Week. Liked it so much I stayed." It feels good, keeping my gaze steely and level while I lie to the man I nearly died to save. Truth is I came here for him. He may as well have been feasting on the marrow of my bones all these years, just like Agent Orange, both of them cancers feeding off what few months I have left.

I study him a minute, decide I made the right choice, coming here. I figure I saved his life, so it's mine to take if I choose.

"Yeah, it's a good town for bikers." He pets his goatee as if it were a dog.

"Crankshaft!" hollers a barrel-chested man from the far end of the bar. "We rollin'?"

The lieutenant lifts his chin toward the man, then looks at me and smiles. "Walk out with me."

I stand, and the stump of my calf tingles against the boot prosthesis. Lieutenant Finnegan throws his arm around my shoulders as we walk toward the door.

"We'll have to catch up, now that you live here, Fuzz. I'll show you around, introduce you to my posse."

The warm, salt-scented breeze dampens my skin as we step from the bar into the late-night air, and I draw it into my lungs, lick the briny taste from my lips. "You got a posse?" I know he rides with Night Fiends, but I don't know how many members he keeps at his side. I follow him to his bike, and when he reaches it, he strokes the leather seat, turns to me and grins.

"Twenty-ten Fat Boy Lo," he says. "I usually trade up every year, but this one's a keeper."

"That a leather-covered fuel tank?"

His shaved head nods on his stump of a neck. "You can touch it."

I don't.

He reaches into his saddlebag and pulls out a leather vest, then shoves his meaty fists into the armholes. He holds out his arms, turns slowly to model his colors. Full-patch Night Fiend. When he faces me again, he grins.

I swallow against the hate in my throat. "You ride with the Fiends?"

His snide laughter shoves me backward four decades. "Ride with 'em? Hell, I'm prez of the NSB chapter."

My eyes plow the patches on the front of his vest. *Crankshaft. President. 1%. Vietnam Vet. POW/MIA. Respect Few, Fear None.* Then I see it. *Valor*—the Medal of Honor.

My award.

He wears a patch—not the medal, at least—but it bears the same emblem. I shove my hands into my pockets where they curl into fists.

He must have followed my stare, or else my hatred stabbed a hole into his chest. He clears his throat. "Look, Fuzz—"

"Don't call me that," I say through a vise of teeth.

"All right." His words come out slow, and I know he's measuring me. "We oughta put this thing to bed. We're not dumb kids anymore. I know you believe what you *think* happened, but I was there, too. You took a gash to your head. You weren't thinking right."

The muscles in my jaw clench, and time stretches enough for me to see, without turning, the three Night Fiends standing a dozen yards away, watching us. Watching me.

"If you want, we can talk about it." His voice grows soft, like the lob of gut hanging over his belt. "Sometimes it helps to talk."

I glance at the sky, see the last stripe of sun's fire streak through blue suede. Red sky at night, soldier's delight. I look back at him, squint as if I'm in pain. "Alone."

His eyes glitter in the neon glare. "There's a place on the county outskirts, a dive called Digger's. They close early tonight, but I know the owner. We'll get a bucket of beer, sit out back, talk 'til daylight."

I nod.

It doesn't feel right to straddle my bike without wearing my colors, so I pat my saddlebag to honor them. My patch only has one rocker, but that'll change tomorrow. Cancer's numbered my days, so I'm taking the shortcut to full patch.

I follow the lieutenant out of the parking lot. He rides the double yellow lines, waiting for me to pull alongside. I stay behind, keeping his Fiends patch in the glare of my headlight.

Front Toward Enemy.

I picture how it will go down tomorrow, how I'll throw the lieutenant's vest on Thor's table at the back of the Thunder Hog's clubhouse. The vest will land with the words *Crankshaft* and *President* faceup, and when Thor picks it up and sees the Night Fiends patch on the back, his black beady eyes will come out from under their hoods to gape. He'll stand, shake my hand, pull me against him, and pound my back. He'll say something wise. "Welcome to the brotherhood."

The brotherhood.

Brotherhood.

Time slides around the word, turns it into an echo, and it bounces against the top of my brain like a helium balloon, overinflated and out of reach.

Thor, the Thunder Hogs president, will hold up the vest for other members to see, and he'll smile big and proud. They'll nail Finnegan's cut to the wall over Thor's table. Then I'll get the full patch, not just the probate's rocker

like I have now, says *Thunder Hogs*. And on the front,
they'll put a lightning bolt, because I've killed for my colors.
Respect Few, Fear None. The badge of a killer. I'll ask
Thor—no, I'll tell him—I'll tell him before he nails the
lieutenant's cut to the wall, I'll tell him I want the *Valor*
patch for my own cut. It belongs to me. I earned it.

Now the lieutenant shoots through a red light, and I
know he thinks I'll stay behind, await the green. His head
ducks and tilts to the right as he checks his side mirror,
but I stay on his tail. Laws don't apply to one-percenters
like us, but he don't know I'm a Thunder Hog.

We pull into the small parking lot, and I dismount.
Broken raw-bar oyster shells scattered on the sand crunch
like brittle bones beneath my boots.

"Go on around back," he says. "I'll grab the beer before
Digger locks up." He grins like he's my savior. "It's on me."

Behind the joint, six picnic tables sprawl at odd angles,
and I straddle the bench of the one farthest back, the one
hidden in the shadows of a live oak's dripping moss.
Outside the ring of yellow light splayed by bare bulbs, I
blink fast, force my eyes to adjust. I finger the slim leather
holster beneath my T-shirt, feel the Ka-bar knife tucked
there. She's been with me since Vietnam, came with me
aboard the chopper the day I lost my foot. The day I saw
the Claymore propped on its spindly praying mantis legs.
Front Toward Enemy. The day I shoved Lieutenant
Finnegan over the bank to save his life. The day they pulled
eleven steel balls out of my legs, my stomach, my chest.
The day my head hit a boulder and my skull opened,
pouring out the last drop of loyalty I had for my lieutenant,
my unit, my country.

The lieutenant thumps two buckets of beer on the picnic
table, and a kamikaze ice cube shoots across the table and
lands in the sand on the other side. He sits down across
from me, and his weight shifts the table. He pulls out a

knife, a Ka-bar like mine, pries the top from a bottle, and shoves it my way. I can't help but grin. I pull out my own Ka-bar, slap it against the table in front of me.

He laughs. "Too much alike, my brother." He holds out a fist.

I knock my knuckles against his, though we're nothing alike, and we sure as hell ain't brothers no more. I look up into the tree, stare until I make out scraps of blue night against the groping fingers of leaves.

"You been rolling long?" he asks.

I pull a few swallows from my bottle, wipe my mouth on my hand. "Since I learned to walk again." I stomp my boot in the sand to remind him, and the prosthesis shoots a tingling jolt into my knee. He looks away, doesn't speak for a full minute. I wait him out.

"I told what I saw," he finally says. "What I knew to happen."

"Tell it to me, then. I want to hear you say it."

When he looks at me, his stare is hard, but then it goes soft. He turns away again before he talks, remembering. Remembering the things he made up, not remembering the truth.

I know the truth.

"You were on the bank above me. I looked up, was going to tell you to get the hell down from there, but before I could say a word, you jumped spread-eagle. You were airborne over my head before the mine exploded." He shakes his head. "No idea to this day where the VC were hiding. Hell, maybe they didn't have a clacker. Maybe you tripped a wire."

I can't pry my teeth apart, so I talk through them. "Didn't trip no wire."

He pulls another swig from his bottle. "Clacker, then. They pressed a clacker, set off the mine."

"Clacker. Yeah, I'm sure of that. I saw the Claymore."

Close enough to read the embossed words: *Front Toward Enemy.* "They didn't even try to hide the thing."

"Really," he says. It isn't a question.

"Sitting out there in broad daylight. You walked right past it. That's how come I know there weren't no wire." I stare at him hard. "I shoved you over the bank, jumped right behind you. Musta been in the air when they blew it."

No way can I forget, though I wish to God I could. It was the day I first slid time around. I slowed it down while I was falling through the gray mist. I drew in a full breath, smelled the mud-thick air, and saw my boot fly past my face, hit the ground and bounce. Didn't know then my foot was still in it. I saw the low boulders in my landing zone. They weren't the granite-gray rocks of the West Virginia farm where I grew up, and no moss grew on them, despite the dank. These big stones shined white, like smooth, bleached bones coming out of their graves among leaves and ferns. I slowed time enough to turn, look toward Lieutenant Finnegan, his face buried in the ferns, his hands covering the back of his head.

I heard the crack as much as I felt it. It sounded like a shotgun, but I knew it was my skull breaking open. I stayed awake. Had sense enough to tell the lieutenant to get my boot when I saw my foot was missing.

And he says I misremember.

He works at his bottle now, picks at the label on the neck, peels it loose. "You didn't shove me," he says, low and quiet-like. "I was already down there. You came flying over my head, landed in the rocks." He pushes his empty aside, pulls another bottle from the bucket.

I take the bottle from his hand, surprised that I already have my Ka-bar pointed toward him. I flip off the cap, shove the bottle his direction. I hear him swallow before he ever lifts the beer to his lips.

"Thanks," he says. He pulls a long swig, then he stares off toward the bar as the only car in front of it comes to life, spins shells and loose gravel as it hits the highway. "I carried you out of there."

"You did." I run my finger over the blade.

"You remember that, too?"

"I do. Stayed awake until they loaded me on the chopper." He nods. "Your eyes were open some. Closed some."

"Hard to keep 'em open. Had a hole in my head. No foot." I scrape the back of my hand with my knife, shaving hair, fine pieces of me falling to the table. I blow them away.

"You think I don't deserve it?" He touches a thick finger to the Valor patch.

"Never said that."

"You tried to fight it. I know you called the captain and the major. Said it was yours."

"I shoulda had one. I saved your life, probably some of the other men, too. Nearly cost me mine."

He sucks deep of the night air, and it feels like he pulls it from my lungs. "I saved *your* life," he says. "Carried you to that chopper, bullets whizzing all around, grenades blowing craters at my feet."

"You did. I know. And I thanked you for it. I thank you again." I glare at him until he looks back at me. "But all that happened *after* I saved your life. After I pushed you down the bank. I coulda jumped, left you up there, let you get blowed to bits. That split-second it took me to push you first liked to have killed me." My calf tingles, tries to sleep, so I throw my leg over the bench and stand.

He clears his throat. "You know . . . you gonna live here, we'll cross paths a lot, small town and all." He jerks his head toward the bar's parking lot. "Especially if you ride." He gazes over his shoulder for a while, then turns back to me. "You could ride with the Night Fiends. It takes a while to patch-up—years, sometimes—but I can get you past all that. Have your full patch in two or three months. Prez has powers like that, you know. I say what's what."

I pull another beer from the bucket, flip off the cap with my Ka-bar, keep her in my hand as I guzzle half the bottle. I stare at him. "Been riding some with Thunder Hogs."

The proud look on his face melts, and I want to laugh, but I don't.

"They're a mean club," he says. "Rivals. Might want to think twice before you start hanging around with them."

"Oh, yeah?" I stare at the patch. It's stitched of golden thread with "Valor" embroidered in blue, the same colors as the Medal of Honor. The one he lied to get. The one he took from me.

He nods, presses his lips into a line. "Got to fight your way in, you join the Hogs. Can take as long as four, five years to go full-patch. That is, if you make it that long. The Night Fiends . . . we're a real brotherhood. All for one, one for all. Like we were in 'Nam."

Time slips again, and I see his lips, still wet with beer, slide around the words. *Brotherhood . . . Like we were in 'Nam.* The emptiness in my chest swells, constricts, aches.

"Look here," he says, and he tugs on the Valor patch. "You can't stop staring at the damn thing, can you? If it means that much to you, you can have it. It ain't the real medal, no how." He slides his Ka-bar under the stitches, starts to pop the patch loose.

"Stop it!" Time slips again, all slick and smooth, and I can't seem to wrestle it back into place, make it hold still. It slips backward, and I see the Claymore. *Front Toward Enemy.*

The lieutenant chokes out a wheeze as time glides back into the now, and I find myself twisting his arm at a crazy angle behind his back, my Ka-bar resting flat against his throat. I turn him loose, the broken arm falling heavy toward the sand, and he bends over, vomits on the ground. Beside the acrid beer-puke lays the splattered Valor patch. Stolen from me again.

I hover above him, angel of death or angel of mercy, I ain't sure which. I imagine the Ka-bar sinking handle-deep into the Night Fiends patch on his back. Imagine him breathing his last, his chortling sound, and I'll wonder for a minute if he's laughing. He'll cough then and spray the sand red.

"Brotherhood." I spit on him now, lying in his stench, his puffy bug-eyes looking up at me. "Ain't no such thing." I lean over him, and he whimpers when I snatch the bandana hanging from his pocket. I use it to wipe my Ka-bar, sheathe her at my hip.

I've turned off Route 44 onto I-95 before I realize I've left my colors in the saddlebag. I pull to the side of the interstate, take out my vest and crush it against my nose, breathe deep the animal smell of leather, of things long dead and better for it. I fling it over the guardrails where it lands among the spiky palmettos, and I point my bike again toward the blue mountains of home.

All Grown Up

Daddy says it's a good year, says demand for coal is high, so two cardboard boxes, instead of one, perch on the overstuffed black vinyl couch, waiting for Momma to wrap them. Two birthday presents for me. Momma says it's a double bounty of goodness bankrolled on Daddy's weary shoulders.

Momma wraps the presents in layers of white tissue paper, each layer folded and taped separately, so I'll have to peel away the layers one at a time to reach the goodness inside. She wraps the boxes while I make the icing for my birthday cake. German chocolate with coconut-pecan icing. It's mine and Uncle Bobby's favorite.

I turn ten today at exactly 10:28 p.m., and even though it's not quite noon, Momma said we can count it like I'm ten already, so I can finally use the stove by myself. I stir the pitcher of fresh cow's milk, swirling the yellow cream into the milky whiteness, then I pour it into the big measuring cup. I step down off the stool to level my eyes with the red lines on the glass.

"Use the heavy-bottomed saucepan," Momma says as

she peers through the pass-through between the living room and kitchen. "Keep the heat low, so the milk won't scorch." She smiles and disappears, and in a moment, more tissue paper rattles.

Momma almost didn't let me make my own birthday cake, not because I'm not a grown-up (because I am), but because she said it ain't right to make your own birthday cake. But I wore her down, and a while ago she handed me the wooden spoon with the scorched tip (I burned it last year when I was young), and she told me to be careful with the flame.

I pinch off a wad of the sticky white coconut strings and shove them into my jaw, before I dump the rest of the bag into the icing mixture. I hum "Happy Birthday" because today is going to be the best birthday ever.

"Momma," I call. "You know what? I'm going to be the best cook in all of West Virginia. Maybe in the whole wide world!"

"You think so?" she says from the living room. "I think so, too. You can be anything you want to be, pretty girl."

Momma didn't say, "You can be anything you want to be *when you grow up*." That's because I'm ten. I'm a grown-up now. I hum some more.

I finish cooking the icing, and I smear the thick, sweet-smelling mixture over each layer, then stack them together and cover the top and sides. The church ladies don't put icing on the sides of their German chocolate cakes. Me and Uncle Bobby like our cakes covered up with it, so I made extra. I scrape the bowl and lick the spatula clean, then I see a few bald patches where the cake shows through. I don't think anyone will pay attention to it, and they won't notice that the cake's a little bit lopsided, either, because it's going to taste so good.

Momma dusts her hands together. "There. That's done."

I step around the corner and gawk at my presents, their boxes so pretty wrapped in layers of white tied with pink yarn.

Two presents.

I haven't asked for anything this year, because it never matters what I ask for—I always get what Momma thinks I need. Shoes, or a nightgown, sometimes a church dress. Today might be different, because two presents mean double the chance for something grand.

The trailer shakes when Daddy comes inside and slams the back door so it'll latch. His heavy footsteps tingle through my sock-feet as he ambles up the narrow hallway. "Sure smells good in here, Susie-Q." He grins as he sinks into his armchair, then he catches Momma's eye. "You reckon we can see what's in these pretty boxes, Momma?"

Momma's whole face smiles when Daddy winks at her. "I think so." She snaps a fresh blue cube onto the top of her new Insta-Matic camera.

"Go ahead," Daddy sweeps a big hand toward the presents. "Open 'em up."

Winter wind whines at the door, and I shiver as much from happiness as from the chill in the house. I curl my hands into the sleeves of my sweater and huddle on the floor near Daddy's feet. He raises enough to reach the first box, the biggest of the two, and places it on my lap.

It's heavy.

"Hold up," Momma says. "I need to take your picture, first." She says she likes to record the good days.

I curl my sock-feet beneath me, sit back on my heels, heft the heavy box into the air, and grin. "Cheeeese!"

The flashbulb pops, and black and red circles jump around inside my eyes, and I can't see too good. I blink hard a few times, and the room returns to normal colors again. "Now?" I ask.

"Go ahead, honey." Daddy winks gray-green at me from behind his thick, black-framed eyeglasses.

I want to tear open the layers, uncover the treasure beneath, but I look at Momma and carefully slide one finger beneath the cellophane tape like I've seen her do, then I hold my breath until the tape pops its release. I'm ten now, so I need to open packages like a lady, not a banshee.

Three layers later, I find the thick box beneath the white tissue paper, and I lift the lid. More tissue paper. I shove it aside to uncover a nest of mixing bowls, red, yellow, and blue—and a brand new wooden spoon (no burned tip) lying alongside them. "Oh, Daddy! Momma!" I swipe at the water in my eyes. "Thank you so much!"

I lift out the bowls, each one separated from the others by squares of thick, blood-colored paper I will use later for carpeting in the Barbie dollhouse I made from cardboard boxes. I arrange the bowls in a pretty line, littlest to biggest, across the top of the coffee table. "I've never seen anything so grand," I whisper.

The mixing bowls make me want to cry, but even if my eyes water, I don't cry, because crying is for babies. This is the kind of present a grown-up gets. A grown-up, smart lady who can use the stove all by herself.

"You have another present, Susie-Q." Daddy's voice has a laugh in it, and he hands me the second box. It's almost as heavy as the first.

I sniff and blink fast. This time I open the box like a banshee. Breath whooshes out of me when I lift out the things I needed the most, but didn't know it. Two thick, heavy, cloth-bound cookbooks: *How to Cook – Volume I* and *How to Bake – Volume II.*

I squeal and hold up the green books, one in each hand, their weight evidence of how important they are. Before I can scramble to my feet to hug Momma and Daddy, someone pounds at the front door, and we all turn.

Momma and Daddy look at each other, and I don't understand what the look means, but my belly feels like fish are swimming in it, so I know something is bad. None of us moves, then the knock comes loud again.

"You don't think. . ." Momma puts a hand to her mouth.

"He'd better not." Daddy's face turns hard like a statue's. Momma's face looks white, like when she first powders it, but she's not wearing makeup today.

Daddy stands, steps across the strewn sheets of tissue paper, opens the door.

"Where's my birthday girl?" Uncle Bobby's drawl oozes across the living room, and I leap to my feet and run toward him, my arms reaching for him before I get there. He grins, and his blue eyes sparkle like the fancy earrings I saw in the *Sears Christmas Wish Book*. Uncle Bobby scoops me off the floor with one arm and spins me around and around. If I close my eyes, I'll fly away, so I keep them open, because I don't want to miss one second. Now that Uncle Bobby's here, it really is the best birthday ever.

When Uncle Bobby slows the spinning, I bury my nose in his neck, smell his Aqua Velva, his Camels, and his Kickin' Chicken. One of his girlfriends said he smells like raw maleness, which has to smell nasty, but I think he smells like a handsome man. Uncle Bobby sets me back on the floor, but my head thinks I'm still up in the air. I love him in ways I can't name.

Uncle Bobby grins at Momma and Daddy, but they don't act happy to see him. I follow where Daddy's hard stare is looking, and that's when I see the bottle in Uncle Bobby's hand. Maybe my seeing that Kickin' Chicken bottle—which really has a picture of a turkey on it, not a chicken, and the turkey is standing still, not kicking— maybe my seeing it gave it some kind of power, because it lifted right to Uncle Bobby's lips without him even looking at it. He finished all that was left of it, then wiped his lips on the sleeve of the splotchy Air Force jacket he brought back from Vietnam.

He holds the bottle out to Momma. "Throw this away for me, Sis."

Momma's lips melt into a thin white line, but she takes the bottle from Uncle Bobby's hand and flings it hard into the trash can. When the bottle shatters real loud, something thuds against the inside of my chest.

"Bobby," Daddy finally says, and I hold my breath. "Didn't think we'd see you today."

Uncle Bobby smiles at me, and I breathe. I'm flying again.

"What?" he says. "You think I'd miss my best gal's birthday?" Uncle Bobby tilts to one side, like the wind is about to blow him over, but I look at the curtains, and they're holding still. He stands like that for a minute, kind of sideways, and I think he looks a lot like my birthday cake: sort of lopsided, but still pretty.

It's then I notice that Momma is watching me look at him. She smooths a wrinkled sheet of tissue paper on her lap, folds it into a neat square. "I reckon you can stay for a piece of cake, Bobby. Susie made it herself."

Uncle Bobby gawks at the cake, then looks at me with bug eyes, then gawks at the cake again and licks his lips. "German chocolate? That's my favorite." His words come out slow and thick, like the icing when I stirred it in the pot.

"Mine, too, Uncle Bobby! That's how come I made it."

"Oooh-wee! Sure does smell good." He flattens his hands on the kitchen table and twists his face toward the cake, sniffing loudly. I don't know if he loses his balance, or if the table won't hold a man as big as a mountain, but the table tilts, and the cake slides toward Uncle Bobby as Uncle Bobby slides toward the floor.

"Good God!" Daddy yells. He rushes at Uncle Bobby, too late to save him. Daddy shoves his hands under Uncle Bobby's arms, hefts him from behind. I think Uncle Bobby is too big and too heavy, but Daddy hauls him up like I haul Raggedy Andy, and he plants Uncle Bobby on his feet.

Uncle Bobby chuckles. "Whoops!"

His eyes warm my face, and I know he's grinning his

pretty white-teeth grin, but I can't look at him. I can only see my first-ever German chocolate cake—my first-ever cake at all—splattered on the floor like a fresh cowpile.

"I think it's time to go," Daddy says. His voice sounds a way that makes me shiver.

"Awww, now, don't be like that. It was an assident." Uncle Bobby's word has S's that don't belong.

Daddy's eyes look like flint rock, and I worry they'll catch afire. "You heard me," he says.

Uncle Bobby's pretty lips curl into an ugly snarl, like the neighbor's Bluetick hound before it bit me last summer. He points his finger at my daddy, and I close my eyes, using my only birthday wish to take away that pointing finger. But then I remember I don't have a cake to wish on, so I open my eyes. I want to scream that it was an *accident*—I want to say the word the right way, so Daddy will understand.

"You ain't treated me right since I came home from the war," Uncle Bobby says.

Daddy doesn't blink. "I said it's time to go." He sits again in his chair, and I know everything's decided and settled.

A snort shoots out of Uncle Bobby's nose, and he looks at Momma. "You gonna let him talk to me like that, Sis?"

Momma's face freezes, turns hard and bright pink, like it does when I'm in big trouble. "You heard him, Bobby."

Uncle Bobby's face twists up in a way that scares me a little bit. Not like a little kid would get scared, but like a grown-up gets scared, because I think Momma's a little bit scared, too. Uncle Bobby puts his arm around Momma's waist and pulls her up against him. He grabs her other hand in his, and he's dancing with her.

"Just a spin around the floor, little sister. It's a party, ain't it?" He kisses Momma sloppy on the mouth, and she pulls away and smacks his cheek real hard.

Daddy jumps up again, and this time he grabs the collar

of Uncle Bobby's jacket and whirls him around. Daddy cocks his fist beside of his head, and that fist is a gun aiming to go off. Momma puts her hand on Daddy's arm, and Daddy's fist wilts. He lets go of Uncle Bobby's jacket, then he turns, opens the front door and stands beside it.

Uncle Bobby turns to me. "Susie, I have to leave, darlin'. But you remember . . . it ain't because I want to."

I stand up when he starts toward me, his arms ahead of him to give me a goodbye hug, but his big hands are too heavy, and their weight carries him forward too fast. He stumbles off-kilter into the coffee table between him and me. My pretty mixing bowls fly into the air, and I stretch to reach the blue one, but it's too far from my fingers. The floor catches and scatters red, blue, and yellow chunks.

Momma's face rests in her hands, so she can't see what's happening. Her shoulders bounce, and I can almost hear her crying. My legs aren't strong anymore, and they try to stop working, so I sit down hard on the floor. Uncle Bobby lays spread across the pretty broken pieces of my birthday.

He lifts his head off the floor, and his eyes find me. He looks sad and ashamed, and I reckon I should feel sorry for him, but nothing in me wants to do that. When Daddy helps Uncle Bobby stand, little pieces of my bowl are stuck to his jacket. I've never noticed before that Daddy is taller than Uncle Bobby.

Uncle Bobby's lip is bleeding, and it takes some of the pretty out of his smile. "I'm sorry, Susie. I'll get you another one." He watches Momma pick up the pieces and drop them into the cardboard box they came in, then he dusts the little pieces from his jacket and gives me a funny look.

"No, don't give me nothing."

"What was it, anyway?"

I shake my head. He can't ever give me back what they were. They were the prettiest mixing bowls in the world, a grown-up present bankrolled on Daddy's weary shoulders.

Worth Fighting For

Clinton came from good quarreling stock. William and Macie Slade's bickering, arguments, and barbed debates were the stuff of local legend. After one infamous fight in which his mother had thrown a whole roasted chicken at his father's head, Clinton had asked his father why he didn't just leave and marry someone he could get along with. William had backhanded his thirteen-year-old son so hard that Clinton's jaw momentarily disengaged, and blood spurted from his lip—the only time his father had ever hit him.

"I took a vow before God!" his father growled, voice full of venom. "'Til death do us part." William shrugged off his anger like a wet coat, swiped the blood from Clinton's chin with a flick of his finger and winked. "Besides, why would I leave the devil's daughter, only to marry his sister, instead? All women are wicked, son, but it's a blessing to marry one, and a duty to stay with her."

Clinton sucked his bleeding lip, wondering if marriage was God's blessing or His curse. He was too smart to ask.

That night, Clinton counted out the months between his parents' anniversary and his birthday, discovered they must have conceived him in a fit of passion. He was William and Macie's only child. Their *love child*.

A smile now tugged Clinton's lips at the twisted memory.

"Stop smiling, Clinton. It's not funny," his wife Paula said from across the kitchen table. "I can't stand their constant warring. We should drive into town and get a room. I can't put up with it all weekend. I told you this would happen." She huffed. "We should have made a reservation before we left home, like I said."

Clinton glanced at his mother, then closed his eyes. Didn't Paula realize she sounded just like them? Is that why he'd married her, the familiarity of conflict?

Macie yanked the dish towel from her shoulder and threw it onto the Formica tabletop, where it knocked over Clinton's nearly empty coffee cup, spilling the dregs in an ugly brown stream across the table. "William, turn down that blasted television! I can't hear myself talk."

The Ben-Gay commercial spouting from the living room quieted a decibel. "That ain't stopped you yet," William yelled.

Macie slid the Bundt pan onto the wire rack, slammed shut the oven door hard enough to vibrate the table. "Shut your trap, old man!"

Paula's over-plucked brows formed severe angles as she leaned again toward Clinton. "You know they're miserable. Do you think they'd get a divorce if we paid for it? Maybe they just can't afford it."

"For God's sake, Paula." Clinton yanked the damp towel from the table, carried it to the kitchen sink, rinsed it and draped it over the lip of the sink. His parents' relentless bickering was the one thing he could count on. He had no idea why or when they'd started arguing, but it had gone on for as long as he'd been alive. Sometimes he'd caught them grinning at one another during a heated fight, as if they enjoyed it. Nearly fifty years of marriage, and their relationship never changed. He'd be damned if he'd be the one to change it.

Paula's answer to everything was to walk away. She'd walked away from her ex-husband the night of their first anniversary, from her final semester at college two months before graduation, and from three jobs since Clinton had married her. His marriage was a waiting game—him waiting for Paula to leave him. Maybe he was tired of waiting. Maybe he'd leave, first.

"I don't do drama, and I don't do fighting," she told him on their wedding day. Said nothing in life was worth fighting for, anyway.

Now he stared out the window at the leafless oak, picking out the last few rotting boards that had once been his tree house, his refuge from the brawling. He didn't know how much longer Paula would stay with him before leaving, but he knew he'd never ask her to stay. Maybe he couldn't live happily ever after with his wife, but he didn't want what his parents had, either. It was only after he and his wife moved away from Hillsville for one of Paula's new jobs that Clinton realized he'd made a life of doing things he didn't want to do. Holding on to Paula wouldn't be one of them.

"What's a man have to do to get a drink of water around here?" William called from the living room.

"I guess he has to get off his—"

"Mom!" Clinton said. "Can you and Dad tone it down a bit, just for one day?" He pressed his lips into a thin smile directed at his wife. "I'll bring you a glass of water, Dad," he called.

Paula stood and took a glass from the cabinet, handed it to Clinton. "Told you we shouldn't have come," she whispered as he filled the glass. "It's always the same." She rolled her eyes when the volume of the living room television grew so loud she had to raise her voice to be heard. "God knows why your parents haven't killed each other and ended their misery. Ours, too."

Clinton had heard the comment before, not just from his wife, but from aunts, uncles, the county sheriff, even the preacher at the Methodist church.

"Look at the time," Paula said too brightly. "Mrs. Slade, it's nearly time to leave for your appointment." She winked at Clinton. "I can drive you. Do you want to change before you go?"

Clinton's mother looked down at her calico, snap-front housedress, then fixed Paula in a cool stare. "What's wrong with what I'm wearing?"

Paula shifted, smoothed her skirt. "Not a thing. You look just—lovely. I'll—let me get my coat, and we'll be on our way."

"You stay here and watch the cake," she said to Paula, then shot a warning look at Clinton. "Fifty-five minutes and not a second more, you hear?"

The television went silent. "I'm taking her to the doctor," William called from the living room. "You two came all this way, you don't want to spend your vacation sitting in a waiting room full of germs." He grunted. "My luck, I'll probably catch funeral ammonia from one of them old geezers while I'm waiting on her."

Paula lifted her chin. "Funeral ammonia?"

"Pneumonia," Clinton translated. "The kind that'll kill you."

"Macie Slade!" his father yelled from the living room. "Get a move on. Doc Carson won't wait all day. You ain't that special."

Clinton turned and grasped his mother's arm, reached for an answer to the question he couldn't think to ask. She pulled away, bustled across the kitchen. "Gotta get my purse, before that old fool out there leaves without me."

"Mom, you're seeing Dr. Carson? Why are you seeing Dr. Carson?"

His mother moved faster than her years should have allowed, ducked into the hallway and climbed the stairs away from her son.

"Who's Dr. Carson?" Paula asked.

Clinton pushed past her on the way to the living room. "Dad, why is Mom seeing Dr. Carson?"

William Slade stood by the door, shoving his meaty hands into the same quilted, brown-twill jacket he'd worn when Clinton moved away from Hillsville five years ago. "'Cause he's the one who Doc Fenwick sent her to, I reckon."

"Okay, but why?

"Who's Dr. Carson?" Paula struck an absurdly demanding pose in the doorway between the kitchen and living room, her fingers splayed against the daisy wallpaper in way that made her fingers look like petals, her palm the flower's orange center.

William took a long time fastening the metal buttons on his jacket, his thick fingers slow, certain. "Some test results," he finally mumbled.

Clinton stepped forward, his face a foot from his father's as he parceled out clipped words. "What—kind—of—test."

Pain flashed across William's face, quickly replaced by annoyance as his hands swept the air, missing Clinton's nose by a scant inch. "A test! Some test. Some biopsy something or the other."

"Biop—" Clinton's breath ran out, stealing the word from his mouth.

Macie appeared behind Paula. "Excuse me, please." She stepped past her daughter-in-law, scowled at her husband. "Goodness gracious, William, I thought you'd have started the car by now. You know I don't like sitting on cold leather seats. You should have listened to me and bought a car with those nice velour seats. I never did like leather in a car. Too hot in summer, too cold in winter."

William's eyes found Macie, and he held her in his gaze,

an odd look passing between them that Clinton couldn't decipher. "Just shuddup and get in the car, woman. You'll be late to your own funeral."

Papery lips brushed Clinton's cheek as his mother whisked past. "Keep it up, William, and you'll be early to yours."

The room turned around Clinton, or maybe he turned in the room. He found himself facing Paula, breathless.

She rolled her eyes. "For the last time, Clinton, who is Dr. Carson?"

Clinton carried the suitcases from the trunk of Paula's Lexus into the town's only bed and breakfast. Paula had told him before they'd married that she wasn't a hotel kind of girl, so he'd traded relaxing swims in resort pools and morning workouts in gyms with views for afternoon teas and too-sweet breakfasts with strangers.

She appraised their room, slid a finger down a curtain made from the same silk damask that covered the upper half of the walls, and she appeared to find it suitable. "This is what your parents should do to their house." Her eyes shifted as she licked her lips. "Get rid of those daisies in the living room and the teapot wallpaper in the kitchen."

"Like that'll ever happen."

"Yeah. We'll probably be the ones who'll have to change it."

"What do you mean?"

Her cheeks flushed. "Oh, you know what I mean. Someday. No time soon, of course. You're their only child. You'll inherit their house when . . . you know." She smoothed an imaginary wrinkle in the bedspread. "That's a long time away. Nothing to worry about now."

Clinton flung the larger of the two suitcases—Paula's— onto the bed, skewing the coverlet. "We should be getting back. They'll be home already, and I want to hear what the doctor said."

"What's the rush? Dinner's not for another hour, and if we get there too early, your mom will want to give me another cooking lesson. I'm sure she'll blame that overdone cake on me, too." Her lips twisted to one side. "You can ask them about the test results over dinner. Maybe there'll be less shouting that way."

"It was a *biopsy*, Paula. They sent her to an oncologist. I think it's pretty obvious what the test results revealed." He stood by the rolltop desk, gouged his finger into a hole dug into the wood by a former bored guest. "I'm sure there'll be more to discuss than polite dinner conversation."

Paula tugged at her lip, and for a moment her eyes appeared wet and shiny, and it startled Clinton that she looked like she might cry. She sniffed a deep breath, huffed it out slowly, loudly. "I just wanted a little time to decompress, you know?" She pulled out her cell phone, touched the first number on speed dial, turned her back to Clinton. "Let me check on the store, then we'll go." She spoke into the phone before waiting for Clinton's response.

Clinton sank onto the bed, stared toward the window, unable to see what lay beyond the haziness of the sheer curtain.

"Are you listening to me?"

He turned toward the irritated tone of Paula's voice, more than toward her words. "Yes?"

"Heather's going to cost me the Landers' job by the time I get back down there. She ordered the wrong upholstery pattern, and it won't work with the other tapestries in their study." She rubbed the back of her neck. "Honestly, it's impossible to teach that woman the importance of detail. She never seems to grasp the little things."

Clinton set his jaw. "Why don't you just drive on home? I'll go back and stay at Mom and Dad's, take care of whatever they need on my own. You know you'll be happier." He wanted a fight, needed a fight. He hadn't expected her relieved smile.

"Oh, honey, you're absolutely right, you know? All their

bickering . . . well, it rattles my mind. And that doctor drama, it reminds me too much of Daddy's sickness when I was a child. I can't handle it."

Clinton knew little of her father's "sickness," other than the man had run out on his family and drank himself to death. It hardly seemed the same.

She perched lightly next to him on the very edge of the bed, like a bird ready for flight, and lightly patted his leg. "If you'll get our bags, I'll take care of the front desk." She smoothed a strand of hair back into her French twist and headed for the door. She paused there, delicately sliding her fingertips over the damask wallpaper again, then she strolled out.

Clinton followed. Disappointment pulled the corners of his mouth. What was wrong with this woman? Didn't she realize now was the time he needed her the most? He hefted her overstuffed suitcase into the trunk, part of him wishing it wouldn't be unloaded at home, part of him knowing it would be.

Paula's high heels clicked on the cobblestone, and she touched Clinton's arm. "Thank you for being so understanding about this, Clinton. I really need to make a good impression on the Landers. If she likes my work . . . well, you never know where it could lead." Her smile appeared too tight. "You're a good man."

"I'll just call a cab, Paula," he said when she walked toward the passenger side. "We're so close to the interstate, there's no need to drive me into the country and come back out here again."

"That's silly," she said, pausing with her hand on the car door. "We haven't had an hour alone since we got here. That's no kind of vacation. At least let me ride with you back to your parents' house."

"It's okay. Really. You should get on the road, get home before dark."

She walked back to him. Her quick kiss caught only the side of his mouth, but this time her smile was genuine. "Tell your parents I said goodbye."

Clinton sat in the dawning light of his parents' living room, listening to the too-loud tick of the mantle-clock as the hour approached five. He propped his elbows on his knees, picked at a hangnail. *Stage four.* His mother would start chemo on Tuesday, two days after his scheduled return home. He should stay. He'd call Paula later, tell her his mother needed his help. The time apart might do his marriage good. It'd give him time to think, sort through things, figure out what he was doing with his life. Maybe his discontent with work was seeping into his life at home. He was tired of teaching history to high-school students who didn't believe the past mattered.

He walked softly toward the kitchen, avoiding the creaking board in the living room floor, but he stopped when he heard the crunch of gravel in the driveway. Someone turning around? The paperboy, maybe. He stepped to the window, surprised to see Paula's Lexus. He watched her for a moment, unsure why she'd returned. She sat behind the wheel, looking up at the house's second-story windows. Checking to see if anyone was awake at this hour, he supposed.

Clinton opened the front door carefully, so as not to wake his parents. His father's ratty house slippers sat just outside the door, and he slipped into them. A brisk chill raced across his skin, causing him to shiver.

A relieved smile lit Paula's face when she saw him. The car door chimed when she opened it, and she stepped out and rushed toward him. "How are you, Clinton?" she asked. "I feel so bad about leaving you when I did. I just didn't think—didn't want to believe—well, the news—it's such a shock. How's your mother? Your father? I didn't expect. . ." Her words rolled out on one foggy breath, and she slid her arms around him.

Clinton held his wife, patted her back. He didn't know what to say, didn't think he'd see her until he returned home, wasn't sure she'd even be there when he arrived. "Hey there," he finally managed.

Paula pulled back and looked up at him, her eyes watery despite her smile. "I have some good news." She placed her hands on his chest. "I saved the Landers job, and better still, she referred me to the Reynoldses—you know, that estate home next door to her?—and Mrs. Reynolds hired me on the spot. It'll pay enough for you to take some time off, if you want. Spend it with your mother."

Clinton's mouth opened, then shut, but he didn't speak. He'd thought she'd run away again, yet here she stood in front of him. He'd thought her leaving was selfish, but she'd returned offering precious gifts of time and financial support. Nothing made sense. He rubbed his eyes with his fingers.

She tilted her head to one side and looked at him. "Did I wake you?" Paula took his hand, led him toward the door. "It's freezing out here. Let's get you back inside . . . before you catch funeral ammonia."

She smiled, and even through his confusion, he recognized the burning of his face as shame. It mortified him that he'd seriously thought of leaving her.

He put on coffee while Paula returned to the car to bring in a bag of fruit and a box of pastries she'd picked up at the twenty-four-hour grocery on the way through town. She put the sweet rolls in the oven to warm, and then she and Clinton cut up the fruit, the two of them working in silence.

"She's a fighter," Paula finally whispered as she sliced a red apple. "She'll be okay."

It surprised Clinton to see tears in her eyes. "Don't, Paula. Don't cry." A floorboard creaked overhead, and he pointed toward the ceiling. "We need to be strong for her. No tears, okay?"

Paula swiped at her eyes. "I want to tell you, before they come down. . . . I shouldn't have said what I did about them getting a divorce. They have their own way, I guess. You know . . . how they love each other."

How they love each other. Is that what it was that kept them together? Love? "I don't know," Clinton said. "Forty years ago, divorce might have been a good idea for them."

"You plan on sleeping all day, old man?" Clinton's mother's voice carried through the heat vents. "Get up, lazybones."

Paula's caramel-colored eyes grew round, and she giggled, and despite the bluish fatigue beneath her eyes, Clinton recognized her loveliness. He wanted to tell her how much it meant that she'd made the two-hour drive back, how much it meant for her to stand here with him, cutting fruit at dawn. He wanted so much to tell her he loved her. Instead, he bent and kissed her forehead.

An hour later, Paula and Clinton's father worked the daily crossword puzzle in the living room, and while helping his mother put away the breakfast dishes, Clinton offered to stay another week. She shooed him away. "I've made it this far without you holding my hand, young man. I reckon I can get by a little longer."

Clinton's mother eyed him until he shifted to the other foot. Why couldn't he bring himself to say it? Were those three words really so difficult, so taboo, so foreign in this family that he couldn't say them aloud?

"I love you, too," his mother said, her mouth twisting to one side. "Besides, you and Miz Paula got business at home needs tending."

Clinton wondered what business she referred to—Paula's interior design business, or the business of their troubled marriage? And was it really troubled, or was it all in his mind? If arguing could be interpreted as love, and if leaving meant sweet reunions, how would he ever know?

Two months later, Clinton again sat in his parents' living room. "Mom, you need to stick with Dr. Carson's plan. He knows what's best."

She waved her hand. "He knows what's best for his pocketbook, that's what he knows."

"Don't think of it as four more treatments. Think of it as *one* more. Then after that, one more. You can get through anyth—"

"Don't tell me what I can and can't do, Clinton Slade." His mother seemed as astonished by the sharp tone of her voice as Clinton did. She grew quiet a moment, then removed and rewrapped the paisley scarf around her head.

Clinton blinked hard and turned away from the raw pink nakedness of her scalp. His mother had lost her long, snowy-white hair after the fifth chemo treatment.

"Only so much vomiting a body can take, anyhow," she said quietly. Then she smiled at Clinton. "The people at the hospice place are so nice. The nurse who's going to come here to the house is the kindest, plumpest little thing. A real sweetheart."

Clinton sat straighter, glared at his father. "Dad, say something."

He held out his hands. "What? What is it you want me to say, son?"

"Talk her into it! Make her go." Clinton clenched and unclenched his fists. Of the many times his father should have acquiesced to his mother, this wasn't one of them.

William's eyes puddled. "Let it go, son. Leave her be."

It was the kind and plump little hospice nurse who found them at home and phoned Clinton seconds after she called the ambulance.

"Your father was spooned right up against your mother in the bed," she said. "Hugging her real close, so tight you couldn't get a wedge between them. The empty OxyContin bottle was lying by his side." She made a soft humming noise. "We had to take him in, so we couldn't leave your mother here in the state she was in. They were both alive when they left here in the ambulance, but not by much. You'd better come, quick as you can."

When Clinton and Paula arrived at the hospital two hours later, Paula balked at the door to the critical care unit. "I can't go in there," she said, her lower lip trembling. "I'll be sick."

Clinton fixed his eyes on the door. "Wait in the lobby."

The doctor told Clinton they'd pumped his father's stomach just in time. "If the hospice nurse had found him half an hour later. . ." She shook her head. "They must really love each other. I guess they couldn't bear the thought of being apart." She offered a small, sad smile. "Sharing the poison. Like Romeo and Juliet."

Clinton blinked against the strangeness of her words. "They were married forty years, and they fought like cats and dogs the whole time," he said, and the guilt of airing their dirty laundry at a time like this made his face burn.

The doctor's head tilted a scant inch to one side, and she held her gaze steady on Clinton's face. "Only the most precious things are worth fighting for. Maybe their marriage is more precious to them than you know." She straightened and touched Clinton's arm. "Your father will likely move into a regular room tomorrow. We'll keep him a day or two for observation. Your mother . . . she won't return home," the doctor said. "Today, maybe tomorrow. . ." She took one of Clinton's hands in both of hers, her touch dry and cool. "A chaplain is available to speak with you at any time."

Clinton's tongue thickened, stuck to the roof of his mouth. Beeping sounds from each of the unit's rooms announced heartbeats, continuing life. He nodded, and the doctor patted his hand, then turned and pressed the giant metal button on the wall to open the doors, and she walked out of critical care.

Snow-heavy clouds hung low, and dusk approached as Clinton and Paula pulled into the driveway at his parents' house. "You want me to go in with you, love?" Paula asked.

He stared at her a moment. So many strange words he'd heard today, this last from her lips the strangest. *Love,* she'd called him. "No. I'm just going to grab a few things for Dad. Mom won't need—" He shrugged, opened the car door.

In his parents' bedroom, Clinton stuffed pajamas and a change of clothes into his father's old Army duffle and slung it over his shoulder. He stepped over papery tissues, dry wipes, empty packets left by the paramedics. He turned toward the bed then, saw the nest his parents' bodies had made in the center of the double-wedding-ring quilt his mother had stitched before they were married. She should have it with her.

He picked up the quilt, draped it around his chilly shoulders like a boxer leaving the ring, walked outside, and closed the door of his boyhood home.

Paula stood on front porch steps, crying. Light snow flurried from the sky, tiny flakes settling in her hair, melting on her cheeks. "I'm so sorry, honey," she said, slipping her hand into his.

Clinton sheltered her beneath his blanketed arm, led her to the car, gripped her hand until she wriggled her fingers against him.

Good Friends

She has a great body, my friend does, I'll give her that. And I have no problem telling you she's at least ten years younger than I am, and looks it. Doesn't seem fair that she's got a grown son and still has a flat belly and perky . . . well, you know. I don't talk like that. No sense in mentioning body parts the Lord told us in the Good Book to keep covered.

She don't feel ashamed of dirty talk, though. Every other week or two she says, "ass," or "hell," or "damn," and once she even called Simpkin Dodger down at the bank a peckerwood! She liked to have embarrassed me to death, being as I was the one who told her to start up her accounts there. (They give away a fifty-dollar bond to the one who refers somebody.) No, she didn't call him that to his face. She told me he acted like one, though, and that's enough.

It ain't like I expect her to act ladylike, that one, because I know she ain't got it in her, but a little common decency is called for, especially around the good folks at Rikki's Tiki. See, it was one of them days at Rikki's when she sat across the bar from me that let me know she's got a thing for my man Jackson. She don't hide what she's thinking none too good. Tends to say what she thinks, even when she don't think.

People seem to love her, though, and she soaks up all that attention and affection like a big, soppy-wet sponge. I'd just like a little of her spillovers to trickle my way. My love sponge has been hard and dry for years, yet she don't seem to notice that she takes more than her share of what little love is out there.

Could be the way she was raised. I suspect she wasn't taught no better.

I never met her parents. They live in Atlanta, up in what she calls "the big house." For a long time, I thought she was talking about prison, but she meant one of them mansions like what sits on a postage-stamp yard and costs six or seven digits. They gave her the cottage, which really ain't no cottage at all, but a three-bedroom, two-bath, beach-style house on the inlet. Maybe that's what makes her like she is—you know, wanting everything she sees, like it's owed to her. Like she wants my man.

Well . . . he ain't *my man*, really. I don't *own* him. But ever since me and Jackson went out that time, he's been watching me from the far end of the tiki bar. Keeps eyeballing me, even though when I catch him at it, he looks away in a hurry. The shy type.

My date with Jackson happened way before she started showing up at Rikki's Tiki, wearing her frilly tops and high heels and that fake suntan. She keeps a fake suntan, I tell you. And us living right here at the best beach in Florida where real suntans are free. The way she throws away money!

She came down here because of her boy. He's in school at the aeronautical college, getting some high-in-the-sky degree. My oldest boy should be about his age by now. No, I ain't seen him since he was a tadpole. State of Kentucky took him away from me, gave him to his daddy, my first old man. We kept in touch for a while after I moved away, but then my spiteful in-laws poisoned his mind against me. But *her* boy, he's already learned how to fly a plane! I don't reckon they own one, though. He must be borrowing the ones at the aeronautical school.

Her son takes her to lunch every Wednesday. Or she takes him, I'm not sure which way it works. I envy her that—I admit my flaws, and envy is one—her getting to see her boy regular. I wonder what my boy looks like, if he's tall like his daddy, or short like me. My boy could fly a plane, too, if he had money to go to one of them big colleges. She says her son's gonna be a pilot at a big airline, but he can make more money if he gets his doctor's degree first. I told you she's all about the money, didn't I? Well . . . she is.

That's why she's after my man, Jackson. He ain't rich, mind you, not the kind of rich she's used to, though he comes from good people. Owns a big farm out in Samsula, the one what sells them cows with the camel humps on their backs. He does all right.

Her husband? Oh, he died. Some electrocuting tragedy. That's another thing we have in common, both of our men were zapped. Her man's misfortune probably wasn't as horrible as the one what killed my Luther. I must have told him a hundred times not to play that CD player next to the bathtub. He always said he'd be careful, that a man needs good music to relax him after a hard day. The sheriff kept asking when it was Luther started listening to Prince and The Revolution. Said he hadn't ever heard him listening to anything but country all them years they played poker together. I told him I reckon it was when he got some good sense and cheer about him, 'cause country music is sad enough to make a kitten wail.

Besides, my husband must have been distracted that particular day, probably because we'd been in a big fight about housekeeping and laundry-washing and drinking. I don't hold no grudge against him, even though he did die before he apologized. I figure the Good Lord got the last word on that one.

I'm sidetracked. Let me get back to her acting all flirty with Jackson. See, she owes it to me to leave him alone. I was the first friend she ever had at Rikki's. You know how I am, kind to everybody, a real friendly sort. She walked up here to the tiki bar, trying to keep her balance on those uneven deck boards in her wedges, looking all self-conscious and nervous. I recognized the lonesome and scared in her, just like looking in a mirror, and I talked to her right away. We chatted while Nelson made us a drink—she offered to buy me one, and in the spirit of brand-new friendship, I let her—and then when the band started up, I asked her if she liked to dance, and she sure enough said, "Yes!" She jumped right up there on the dance deck, too, and her not even having her drink yet to cut the awkwardness. That right there ought to told me what kind of flop-house doll she really is.

I give everybody the benefit of the doubt. And look where it's got me. She don't even have a real drink, some nights. Just walks right in, gets her a barstool, orders a Diet Co-Cola with lemon (more waste, since the lemon just decorates her glass—she don't even squeeze it), and then she hops out on the dance deck and shakes it. Most of the time I join her. I hate to see a woman up there alone like that. Makes the place look bad. Oh, sometimes I dance up there by myself, too, but never when I'm stone-cold sober. Besides, people at Rikki's know me. They know what kind of woman I am, that I ain't like her. I'm one of the rare birds who cares what people thinks about them. Reputations are hard to shine, once you've let them rust.

See these fingernails? Rough, ain't they? I'd like to get them fancy stick-ons, but I'd probably just chew on them, too. My nerves make me do it. I ain't one of them crazies or nothing, but I do have my bad days. Bad *nights*, really. My trailer gets too quiet in the dark hours, especially after that rowdy bunch of bikers who live at my end of the park settle down. I thought about getting a dog for company, but that's just more food to buy.

She's got a little lap pooch, did I tell you? She totes it in her car sometimes. Gets its hair styled with bows, as if she needs one more way to throw away good money.

She has her good spots, though they're stretched so far apart you got to look to find them. There's nights she'll pick up my tab, like at the end of the month when she knows times is lean. For a while, I thought it was Jackson doing it, him being secret about our love and all, but when I asked Nelson at the bar, he says no, it wasn't Jackson, it was her. Disappointed me a little, though I know you ain't supposed to look at a gift horse's teeth.

I'll tell you the truth, if you'll keep it to yourself. . . I might not have went out with Jackson again if he'd asked me, even before she came along. No, me and him got along fine. Never had a disagreement. It's just that I can't bear the thought of that floozy digging her nails into a Romeo like Jackson. Oh, he's a romantic. He don't show it, but I know.

Surprised me the first time she bought me a drink like that, because she didn't even tell me before she left, so I couldn't thank her proper. I been meaning to tell her I appreciate it, but things slip my mind more and more nowadays. Besides, once she throws one of her fringy, sparkly pocketbooks up on the bar and starts tap-tap-tapping them dragon-lady fingernails against her Diet Co-Cola glass, even Einstein's train of thought would derail.

That's what happens when you're a looker. You become a distraction. People really don't want you around, like you might think they would. She knows it, too. Sometimes when I'm talking to her here at the bar, she'll get that faraway look in her eyes, and I know she's realized that she's starting to strum my nerves. It ain't long after that 'til she leaves. It's a blessing that she realizes it, yes sir. There's times when she gets here, and she'll see me, and I'll wave, and she'll wave back, and then she'll take a seat on the other side of the tiki hut. Them's the days when I know she's probably feeling too pretty for her own good, and she knows I know it, so she just keeps a bit of distance. Maybe she's a distraction to her own self.

It don't bother me none when she keeps her distance like that. Not all friends are as good of friends as me and her, so it would bother some, but not us. Me and her are tight, like the kids say nowadays.

So as I was telling you, it was one of them days when she sat across the bar from me that let me know she's got heartstrings for Jackson. Well, maybe *heartstrings* ain't the right word, but she was sure getting flirty-eyed with him. See, she was talking with me, and me and her danced with all the girls like we do, and then a few men here and there got up to dance, and I was dancing with Jimmy Lee Hester, and next thing you know, she's sitting at the other side of the bar all by herself. Nursing that Diet Co-Cola. With the lemon.

No, honey, she ain't got nothing for Jimmy Lee, but that's funny to think about. Poor Jimmy Lee has got one of them horse faces with eyes that don't quite look in the same direction at the same time, and she's just too prissy for that. She's always polite to him, though. And she ought to be, 'cause he's a good ol' boy.

What made me know she's after Jackson is the way she looked at him, and him at her. She smiled at me when I came back to my barstool, and then her eyes cut over to Jackson, and he gave her one of them hush-hush looks— you know the kind—the ones that say, "I know what you're thinking, but let's keep it a secret." Yes, one of them. Then they both glanced at me and turned away. I ain't stupid. I can read a look.

Her and Jackson ain't even been on a date for as long as she's been coming to Rikki's. That ought to tell her something. See, me and him hooked up right away. First night I seen him here, he sat next to me right here on this corner—it's my regular spot—and we hit it off. We danced to "I Can't Get No Satisfaction," and when the music slowed and the band played Skynyrd's "Love Don't Always Come Easy," Jackson didn't hurry off the dance deck like some men will. No, he slid that calloused hand around my waist, and we kept right on dancing. Oh no, honey, Jackson ain't the type to rub up against a lady. Leastways not in public. It was all proper for prying eyes. He's a real gentleman, I tell you. A cowboy-type man.

Anyways, I had been here a while before he arrived, so I already had a good buzz going. He couldn't have known that, so he bought me a couple or three drinks, and before you know it, I was stumble-drunk. Told you Jackson's a gentleman, and he proved that to me right off. When he seen I wasn't in any shape to drive, he offered to take me home. I had to ask him to stop somewheres on the way, 'cause my stomach wasn't agreeing with me, and I didn't want to embarrass myself by getting sick in his fancy truck.

Him being a respectable sort, he didn't just pull over at any two-bit convenience store. He took me to Denny's, and after I came out of the ladies', he already had us a table with a little pot of coffee waiting. Bought me breakfast and seen to it that I was okay, and once we'd eaten and I'd sobered up to driving-level, he took me back to Rikki's to get my car, and he followed me all the way to my place, and waited for me to pull into the driveway, just to make sure I didn't get pulled by the law. Now ain't that romantic! Our first date. I'll never forget a minute of it.

You see now why I'm rethinking my relationship with Jackson, in light of the way she's taking a shine to him. I won't fight for no man's affection, even if I need it. I just

don't want him falling prey to someone like her. Besides—
and I'm being honest here, so don't judge me—there's not
much else for a woman like me, except to find the next
good man. Look around us. You don't see too many good
ones left, do you? The best ones are already paired up. I
don't want to settle again.

I reckon I waited a little too long for a special man to
come along. And now at my age . . . well, it's real tough.

She can have her pick of good men. Jackson's a catch,
so I can see why she'd make eyes at him, but if he wanted
her, he would offer to follow her home, like he did me,
now wouldn't he? Guess she just can't take a hint, or else
she's one of them that don't do too well with rejection. I
don't hold no grudge against her. She's got her problems. I
understand what that's like. I can't relate to having plenty
of money, or to everyone I meet smiling at me, acting like
they care about me, but just because her problems are
different than mine don't mean they ain't real.

So I'm here for her, standing by in case she needs me.
Why, if it wasn't for me, Lord knows where she'd be.
Lonesome and alone like me, maybe. No true friends at all.

The Lightness of Water

My daddy didn't hold to our land with white-knuckled fists. No, Ol' Doc Walker spat on the dirt when he left West Virginia behind, telling my sister Violet and me that Chief Cornstalk's curse on the mountain state held more water than all of Big Sandy River.

I didn't want to leave, though at six years old, I held no affection for the land. It was Momma I didn't want to leave behind, freshly buried beneath the newly frosted black earth. I didn't mean to make her die, and I was afraid I'd forget what happened to her if we left her there. I needn't have worried. Nearly every day I recall the thunderclap of gunshot that put a hole through my momma.

It wasn't me who pulled the trigger. I ran out of the house to see the fighting, see the government soldiers in their pretty uniforms, running like scattering ants all over Blair Mountain, shooting the striking coal miners.

When I grabbed the cold metal latch and flung open the door that day, Momma called my name, and I turned back to see her tear loose her skirt from Violet's fat little hands. I ran out the door, and Momma chased me, shouting

I should get back in the house, hide under the kitchen table.

After the fighting stopped, Daddy held Momma to his chest while he cried. He petted her hair and kissed her face over and over. His chest hitched when first Violet then I kissed our momma one last time. We sat beside him and watched the few men left in town dig coffin-deep holes, though there weren't nearly enough coffins to go 'round.

Judge Karnes put his dirty hand on Daddy's shoulder, looked at me, then turned away when he spoke. "Doc, it's time to let us have her."

Daddy shook his head. "I'll do it." He stood with Momma in his arms, kissed her face, then laid her in one of the holes the men had dug. He picked up a shovel, and Violet and I watched while he covered her with the hard, dark dirt. At first dawn, while the frigid air still reeked of black powder, he loaded Violet and me onto the train and headed south to Cades Cove, Tennessee, where he said doctors were needed and appreciated. He said land ain't worth the grief it causes.

Took me fourteen more years to understand what he meant, that he wasn't talking about the land, but the people who latch onto it, who think they own the land, when instead the land owns them. He understood what I've only just learned, that love and grief should be bound to people, not to places.

I don't remember much about our old homeplace anymore. Don't remember much about Momma, neither. I don't recall her hands, or her smile, but I still recollect how her face twisted all strange when the stray bullet hit her chest, how she looked at me and opened her mouth like she needed to tell me something important before she crumpled to the cold ground. She was barefoot. The thing I remember best, see every time I think of her, is her bare feet, their soles black with coal dirt.

*

Now I know the word to go with the look that was on Momma's face, and it is *anguish*. It's the same look I seen on Violet's face when her baby died two weeks ago. That kind of hollow suffering is all I think about on my way back to my little cabin in the Cove.

I skid my shoes against the edge of the porch to scrape off the thick mud, slip out my bare feet, set the shoes by the door. Then I reach into my pockets, pull out two big river rocks, feel their cool smoothness, heft their weight in my hands. I drop them onto to the growing pile by the edge of the porch. There's about a dozen now, each of them dried to dull gray.

I hold my breath and quietly step into the cabin, hoping Johnny might be at his daddy's house discussing the sale of the farm, but my luck never did run true.

"Where's dinner?" Johnny eyes me over his cup of coffee, cold, I know.

I swallow to buy time, hang my coat on the peg by the door. "I'll have it ready in a jiffy." I take Johnny's cup from his hand, pour the last dregs and undissolved grains of sugar into the slop bucket under the counter, manna for the pigs. "You talk to the men at the National Park Service today?"

"I done told you, Lurleen, selling family land is like selling your soul. We ain't about to do it."

I nod and walk into our little pantry, lift the handle of the big iron pot from the hook. My elbow hits the small shelf of books Daddy gave me before he died, knocking off Hawthorne's *House of the Seven Gables,* and it hits the floor with a thud.

"You all right in there?" Johnny asks.

"Fine. Made a mess, is all." When Johnny and I married two years ago, I read to him in bed each night. He pretended to like it, but we knew it was more for me than for him. A couple of weeks ago I started the Hawthorne, but one line I read caused Johnny to bust. *"What we call real estate— the solid ground to build a house on—is the broad foundation on which nearly all the guilt of this world rests."*

Johnny tore the book from my hands and flung it against the wall. He called Hawthorne a fool, told me not to bring that ignorance into his bed again.

Now I put the book back on the shelf, promise myself I'll get around to finishing it, and I hurry back to the kitchen and set the heavy pot on the stove. I stoke the fire, then pour water from one of the metal well-buckets into the pot, steal a glance at Johnny. "Might want to draw some more water before nightfall." I dry my hands on a dishrag, turn and trace a sandy wave on the back of Johnny's head with my fingertip, try to soften him up. "We're about the onliest ones left in Cades Cove. It's not doing me much good to keep studying with the granny-woman, if there ain't no people left to tend up here." I take a deep breath and turn back to the stove. "We move to Nashville, maybe I could go to the university and be a real nurse, like Daddy wanted."

Johnny doesn't say anything for a minute, but then he finally speaks in measured words. "Where you been?"

I hate the way my lies pile up like the rocks by the porch. "Up to the granny-woman's place." When Johnny doesn't ask me what I learned, I know he's on to me.

He clears his throat. "You been at the river again, ain't you?"

I blink real fast and keep my back to Johnny as I slip on my apron, keeping it loose around the small mound of my belly.

"You're a fool to keep watch for her," he says. "She'll be back. Violet don't ever stay gone long. She's been running away like this since you two was kids."

I force my hands to unclench, my fingers to relax. I try to nod, but my head jerks on my shoulders like a ratchet.

"Seems she'd have grown up, by now," he preaches. "She ought to know better. I don't know how nor why Walter puts up with her shenanigans."

The door takes a sudden pounding, and my heart kicks.

"Who the devil comes at suppertime?" Johnny unfolds his tall body from the chair, and I admire his broad shoulders. He's a good man, a hard worker, even if he is a little bull-headed. He's never laid a hand to me, though I know at times he's wanted to.

I didn't want to marry him. Daddy insisted. Said it felt right for his two daughters to marry the two brothers our ages who lived up the road, and Violet had already fallen foolish in love with Walter. I told Daddy no at first, but later that night, he told me consumption would take him before winter broke, and his dying wish was for his girls to marry good men. I married Johnny to please him, but now it is I who am pleased.

Johnny flings open the front door, and the reek of Lyle Gregory rides in on the chilly March wind. "Lyle."

"Where's your daddy at, boy?" Lyle talks like his tongue is too thick for his mouth.

"I don't reckon I know. He don't live here."

"I already know that. I been to his house, and he ain't there. He owes me two dollars, and I aim to collect."

I peer around the corner to see Lyle suck a draw from his moonshine jug and fix Johnny with a tobacco-stained sneer. "He ain't gone off to Nashville to sign his deed over, is he?

"Course not."

"He better not." Lyle points his finger at Johnny. "And you'uns better not, either."

I step back to the stove and bury my nose in my sleeve to block out Lyle's sour stink.

"We got to stick together," Lyle says. "Your great-granddaddy and mine settled this cove over a hunnerd year ago. Eighteen and thirty-five. Our granddaddies was borned here, our daddies was borned here, and we was borned here. And we're gonna die here, ever last one of us. You got that, boy?"

My jaw is tight from clenching my teeth, and I expect Johnny feels the same strain times ten. He hates Lyle Gregory almost as much as he hates the way the man always calls him "boy."

"I told you already," Johnny says, "we ain't selling. Now you got anything else to say 'fore I shut the door? Lurleen's got supper on the stove, and I ain't too kindly when I'm hungry."

Lyle grunts.

"When I see Daddy in the morning, I'll tell him you're looking for him. Now if you don't mind. . ."

I peek around the corner again in time to catch another gust of cold air when Johnny opens the door for the fox-faced man to leave. Lyle drunk-stumbles off the porch, and Johnny shuts the door behind him, then stalks back into the kitchen, sits at the table and props his chin on a fist.

I take the cabbage from the icebox, peel off the leaves one at a time, and fold them into little rolls the way Johnny likes them. My throat tightens with each fold. "They're gonna make this a national park, Johnny. You and Walter and your daddy can't hold out forever. Neither can Lyle Gregory. That money won't lay on the table for long. Soon they'll just up and take this land, and we won't have a thing to show for it."

Family land. I rue the day I ever stepped foot in Cades Cove. All Johnny, Walter, and their daddy ever talk about is the importance of their land. Feels like a millstone around my neck, choking me, drowning me.

Johnny snorts. "Great Smoky Mountains National Park. What's so great about it?"

I glance over my shoulder, see Johnny shake his head. I take a deep breath, try to make my voice soft like dandelion fluff so my words will float into his heart. "It might be good to get out of the Cove, start over."

"We ain't a-going."

I can't blink back the tears this time. I swipe them away before they get out of hand, but the room still blurs through fresh ones. I tilt back my head, gaze at the tightly wound bundles of doctoring herbs drying above the stove: elderflower, boneset, skullcap, goldenseal, ginseng, and the blue cohosh root I dug up, in case Violet didn't birth her baby on time.

"Besides," Johnny says, "you'd hate to miss seeing Violet traipsing up the road eating forkfuls of humble pie when she comes home, wouldn't you?"

I spin around and shoot venom from my eyes before I can stop myself.

"Now, Lurleen, don't look at me like that."

I turn my back, peel off another cabbage leaf and make a small, tight roll.

"I don't mean to be cold. You know I love your sister well enough. But she had no business running away like that. Walter is grieving, too. Now he feels like he's lost both of them, instead of just the baby."

I spear the little roll of cabbage so hard the toothpick breaks. "She didn't run away, Johnny, she got run off." *And I didn't stop her.* I suck in a breath, wish I could suck back my words back along with it.

"Who run her off? You ain't fixing to tell me Walter run her off. He's been all over these mountains looking for her."

I hear the legs of Johnny's chair scrape the floor, know without looking he's turned it so he can watch me, see what I know.

"There's something you ain't telling me. Do you know where she is?"

"I—no." My shoulders wilt like the cabbage I drop into the boiling water.

"Who run her off?"

My lip stings. I'm chewing it raw.

"I ain't asking you again, Lurleen. Tell me who run her off."

I whip around, and my throat aches when I whisper the truth. "Your mother, that's who. Your own mother—she ran Violet off."

Johnny stares at me as if he thinks I've gone crazy. Then he moves his head just a little, shakes it side to side. "Momma never would have done that. Not after—not after Violet's baby died."

My hands open without my meaning them to, and the butcher knife I clutched clatters to the floor. I stare at it a moment, not remembering why I held it in the first place. "She told Violet she was wicked and God punished her with that—with the baby." My eyes start to burn, and I blink faster.

Johnny holds out his palms, and his face goes slack. "But Momma loves Violet like the daughter she's never had—better than me, even."

A little laugh jumps out of my mouth before I can catch it. "Your momma loves nary a soul more than you, and you know it." I try to smile, but my lips won't turn up, they twist the wrong way.

"Oh, now, don't cry." Johnny's arms slide around my shoulders, and he pulls me to his chest, rocks me back and forth.

Once the tears start, I can't seem to make them stop. When the crying and trembling finally slow, Johnny sets the pot of cabbage off the stove, leads me around the table to my chair, then fetches me a ladle of cool water in one of the pretty glasses I save for special days.

"I want to know," he says. "Why d'you think Momma run Violet off? Why did she say those things to her?"

I sip from my glass, set it down, trace my finger along the pansy pressed into its side. "I reckon she was upset over what Miss Hazel said."

"The granny-woman? Why would something that old woman said make Momma act hateful with Violet?"

I stare at the water in the glass, feel the coolness against my hand, wonder how Violet ever stood the cold when she waded into the river. A shiver ripples up my back. "She— Miss Hazel—she said it weren't real. We didn't even bury it, Johnny. Didn't you notice that? There weren't no grave! There weren't no grave, and not a soul noticed it." My throat clenches and hurts. "How can you men go about your business after a baby—after something like that happens— and not even notice there weren't no grave?"

Johnny looks out the window into the back field, where crosses mark the graves of my father and his grandparents. I know he's searching for the soft mound of newly turned dirt that doesn't exist, the missing bouquet of brown, wilted flowers collecting evening dew.

He turns to me. "So where is the baby? If the women didn't bury it, what did you'uns do with it?"

I take a sip of water, but the liquid thickens in my throat. I push the glass away. "Johnny, it weren't no baby."

"What do you mean? Violet was as big as a sow and could hardly walk."

"Yes. She was too big, that's what the granny-woman said. She told me in one of my lessons that Violet was too big, too soon, and that might spell trouble."

Johnny steps closer, puts his fingers under my chin, makes me look at him. "You're talking in riddles. What happened to the baby?"

The rock in my throat breaks loose, and words flood out of me. "Johnny, it weren't no baby! Why won't you listen! It's the worst thing I ever seen. It was a wad of hair and bits of bones and things that looked like big pink grapes and little yellow buds, and the granny-woman made me hold out a blanket to catch it, and when she turned and dropped it into my hands, it broke open and water poured out all over the blanket and onto the floor and—"

I jump from the table, overturn my chair and run out the back door, my hands covering my mouth to hold in my sickness until I reach the cool outdoors.

I fall to my knees on the damp grass, try to pray, try to ask forgiveness, but God is too far away. I promised Daddy I'd take care of Violet. But how could I stop her when all she wanted to do was escape the coming years of grief and shame? How could she walk again through town, with all the women pointing and gossiping about the ungodly spawn that came out of her? She wanted to be with her baby—with whatever it was she had borned. She didn't want to live anymore. Wasn't even living the last days she was alive. Who was I to tell her she must? How could I tell to stay here, when all I want is to leave?

When I finally go back into the house, the goodness shows up in Johnny, and he holds a wet cloth to my head. "I'm so sorry, Lurleen. Why didn't you tell me?"

"How could I?"

"I don't understand. It doesn't make sense. Are you sure what you saw? Maybe some of the herbs—"

"I saw it! Your momma saw it, too. So did Miss Hazel. So did that gossiping biddy Corrine, from the church." I take the cloth from Johnny's hand, sink down in a chair and wipe my face. "I wish I could un-see it."

He sits at the table across from me. "You didn't say anything to anyone about it. Not to me, nor Walter, nor—"

"How can I talk about something I don't understand myself? It's not the kind of thing Violet would want me telling. Too many people know already."

Johnny nods and takes both of my hands in his, rubs my fingers with his thumbs. "Lurleen?" When he looks at me, I ain't sure if the blue pain in his eyes is his, or mine. "If you women didn't bury the—the thing that was supposed to be a baby, where is it?"

My mouth is parched. I long for a drink, but I don't dare touch the glass of water. I don't yet deserve the relief it will bring. I stare at Johnny's hands, folded around mine, and my words come out steady this time, dry as bones. "Miss Hazel wrapped it in the baby blanket Violet knitted. She tied a big rock to it and took it up to Abrams Falls. She said a prayer and throwed the whole bundle into the waterfall."

Johnny studies our hands a long time, too. "And Momma run Violet off over that?"

I shrug off my opinion, tell part of what I know to be fact. "Your momma said God punished Violet for being with child out of wedlock. Even though Violet offered to swear on the Bible that she was pure as fresh-fallen snow on her wedding night, your momma said she must have lain with Walter before they married, else she wouldn't have been so big so soon. She said God gave Violet a goblin-child. Your momma made Miss Hazel drown it, before it hatched."

Johnny shudders and drops my hands. He stands and paces half-circles around the table, first one way, then another. "Why didn't Violet stand up to Momma? Why didn't she give her a piece of her mind?" Johnny stops pacing, stares out the window, grows quiet. After a minute, he turns to me. "You're not looking for her."

"What?"

"You're going to the river, you're looking for that—thing. Walter has been all up and down Little Pigeon River, over the mountain to the Cherokee Reservation, up to Maggie Valley, but you haven't once looked for Violet, because you know where she is." He turns, smacks his hand against the side of the cabin hard enough to make me jump. "Where is Violet?"

Johnny's hands grip my shoulders, and he gently shakes me. "I asked you a question. Do you know where Violet is staying? I'll go tell her that my momma is as crazy as a bedbug. She'll listen to me." He stoops, leveling his sight with mine. "Lurleen?"

I remember Violet's careful, steady stride breaking the current when she waded into the icy rushing water above the falls, and I shudder. I should have stopped her. Or joined her.

"Are you cold? You keep shivering." Johnny heads to the front of the cabin, pulls a quilt from the rocking chair near the fire, drapes it around my shoulders. He squats in front of me. "Lurleen, where is Violet?"

I settle my gaze on him, hope it looks as icy as it feels. "I don't know where to find her."

It is the truth. I figured she'd have turned up by now, but the rocks must have done their job.

Pounding at the door wakes us just before dawn, and when I hear the loud hammering, the shooting on Blair Mountain happens again in my head. I search the floor, trying to find Momma, then my sense returns to me, and I see Johnny springing from the bed. I throw a quilt around my shoulders and hurry out of the bedroom behind him.

Miss Hazel's young niece Mary stands on the porch, several inches of her thin cotton nightgown peeping below the hem of her wool coat. "Miz Lurleen?" The gray light of early morning leaks through the fog behind her as she peers around Johnny. "Miss Hazel needs you."

My stomach stiffens. I haven't seen the granny-woman since that night she prayed over the bundle at Abrams Falls. "Can't she take care of it herself?"

Mary rubs her bony hands over her arms and shivers. "She said you need to see this. For your training, she said. It's Mr. Gregory. The oldest one, I forget his name. He had some kind of spell and fell off his horse and broke his leg.

Bone's sticking plumb out of it. It's a sight. Miss Hazel says you need to come. She needs a extry set of hands." Mary shifts from one foot to the other.

Johnny swings wide the door. "Well, come on in while Lurleen gets her coat and shoes. It's too chilly to stand out there and wait."

My feet are slabs of slate as I trundle to the bedroom to get dressed. I'll tell them I'm sick, maybe. Say I'm coming down with something. But then Johnny'll say Miss Hazel can whip up a medicine tea to help me when I get there. I pull on a pair of Johnny's long johns, slip on a loose dress with big pockets, and follow the girl into the fog.

When Mary and I walk in the door to Lyle Gregory's place, the stench of old sweat, moonshine mash, and wet dogs hits me, and my stomach rolls. I cover my nose and follow Mary beyond the quilt Lyle uses for a bedroom door, and I stand still for a moment as my sight adjusts in the dim light. When I can see a bit, I pull back the flour-sack curtain at the window and tie it in a knot to let in the struggling dawn.

"Mary, you best get along home," Miss Hazel says. "You'll have school in a few hours, so go get you some rest." Her voice ripples and quavers with age.

Mary opens her mouth to argue, but shuts it when Miss Hazel's bushy gray eyebrows lift. Mary backs out of the doorway, letting the quilt fall behind her.

I slip off my coat and open the window a crack, as much to flush out the stink as to let in cool air. "What do you need, Miss Hazel?" I can't take my eyes off Lyle's naked, bloody leg. Blood has spilled out and pooled around it on the bedcovers, dripped onto the floor. I ain't seen this much blood since Momma's chest—

"You can fetch the dishpan of water Mary put on to boil before she went to get you."

Startled, I look up, and she motions toward the big, flower-strewn carpetbag that sits on the floor near the bed.

"And we'll need clean rags and the geranium heads from my bag. Lyle's been hitting the corn liquor, so more of that's all we'll give him for pain."

I do as she said, taking a moment to add another log to the blaze in the fireplace, so the tiny cabin will stay warm despite the open window. Then I carry the steaming dishpan and set it on a chair near Miss Hazel, and she motions me to stand beside her.

"We're going to clean up this wound, then you're going to pull on his foot, while I push in the bone."

My jaw works up and down a few times. "Pull on his foot?"

"Yes'm. You'll grab his ankle, hold fast, and lean back with all your weight." She points to Lyle Gregory's meaty thigh. "They's a muscle up here that draws up when the bone breaks. We got to pull it straight, so's I can push the bone back in there and line it up even-like. Then while you're still pulling on his foot, I'll tie this here broomstick tight agin his leg, so he can't bend it."

Most times, the doctoring don't bother me. I'd gone with Daddy even when I was little, and while my job was to keep Violet busy, sometimes I got to watch and help. Now though, I struggle to keep my stomach inside. "And the geranium?" I ask.

"That'll staunch the bleeding where the bone's poking through. Pluck off the petals and mash them with honey to make a poultice, and we'll lay it on the hole before we bandage him up." She slides a gnarled hand under Lyle's thinning ring of white hair, lifts his head and puts a mason jar to his lips. "Get another swig, Lyle, and make it a big one. It'll feel like the devil's got hold of you when Lurleen pulls on your foot." She sets down the jar and dips one of the big squares of muslin into the scalding water.

I watch, wondering how she can bear plunging her hands into water so hot. She drops the dripping rag across

Lyle's protruding bone, and Lyle sucks in a breath and roars through clenched teeth.

"Hesh up, now. It'll hurt worse 'fore it feels better." She holds the mason jar to his lips, and this time Lyle takes long, loud gulps.

I dig around in Miss Hazel's bag until I find one of the cotton-wrapped bite sticks she'd whittled, and I hand it to her.

She smiles, reveals the two gaps where teeth used to be. "You learn real good, Lurleen. You're going to make a fine granny-woman someday. Ol' Doc Walker would be proud." Her eyes start out kind, but they accuse me just before they settle on my belly. "You feeling all right?"

I nod and look away.

Miss Hazel swabs around the bone that sticks out of Lyle's leg, then she hands me the bloody rag.

"Rinch it out good, and hand it back."

My hands light afire when I dip them into the scalding water.

"Seen Violet yet?"

I plunge my hands deeper, now needing the burn. How could I have watched her wade deeper, deeper into the river? "No, I an't seen her." I would have wanted the same thing, the same end to the ache, wouldn't I?

I rinse the muslin, watch the water turn red and sluice between my fingers. I wring out the rag, then offer it to Miss Hazel.

She shakes her head. "Again, 'cept this time leave it wetter. The hot water draws out the 'fection."

I sink the rag beneath the surface of the bloody water. *Water draws out the infection.* This time I wring the muslin gently, just enough to keep it from dripping. When I turn to hand it to Miss Hazel, her stare stabs into me.

"You know what Walter's momma said weren't the truth, don't you? Violet didn't do nothing wrong to cause what happened to her baby. She ain't the onliest one to birth a thing like that. It weren't no goblin."

I can't speak for fear of crying.

A slight shrug lifts Miss Hazel's shoulder, then she drops the rag onto Lyle's leg, bringing another loud growl from behind the bite stick he clamps between his teeth. She dabs at Lyle's leg, then hands me the rag. When I reach for it, she grabs my hand.

"What happened to Violet's baby ain't a-going to happen to yourn. Just get that thought out of your head."

It takes me a minute to swallow. I never told her I am with child.

She points to the end of the bed. "Now go down there and get ready to grab Lyle's foot."

It only takes a minute or two to set Lyle Gregory's leg, but it seems like an hour, because he curses and screams ungodly all through it.

Full daylight shines through the window when we finish with Lyle and get him settled down again. I wash and wring out the bloody rags, hang them on the porch railing to dry. When I come back inside, Miss Hazel offers me a small tin.

"When you didn't come up to learn doctoring with me, I knowed you must be feeling poorly." She studies my face. "There's catnip, peppermint, lavender, and goldenseal in here. You got some 'seng root at home?"

"Yes'm."

"Add a thumb-sized piece to a teacup of water, boil it nearly dry, then add another teacup full of water and steep these here herbs with it. Put a few spoonfuls in a glass of water, and drink it morning and night. You'll feel a might better in a day or two."

My hands tremble as I take the little box. "Did Violet drink this, too?"

Miss Hazel takes one of my hands in hers and pats it. "No, 'cause I didn't give her none. This ain't for the baby,

Lurleen. This is for the momma." Her raven eyes nearly disappear inside her wrinkles when she smiles.

"Thank you, Miss Hazel." I stuff the tin into my dress pocket, pull on my coat and open the door. I turn to look at her. "Bertha's baby should be coming along any day now, shouldn't it?

Miss Hazel's mouth sags. "It was stillborn. I didn't see nary a need to send for you." She touches my arm. "That don't have no bearing on you, neither, Lurleen."

My heart sinks heavy toward my belly. "Violet first, now Bertha makes two," I whisper. "They come in threes." I walk out the door and down the wooden steps.

Miss Hazel steps onto the porch and calls after me. "Lurleen, you drink that tonic, hear?"

I start up the road toward home. The weight in my belly seems to grow heavier with every step, and by the time I reach home, I can hardly walk. I need to tell Johnny I'm in the family way, before he learns it on his own. I need to tell Johnny lots of things, but first we have to get out of Cades Cove. If he learns I'm with child, he'll never let us leave.

When I mount the steps to our cabin, the door opens, and Johnny steps out.

"Good. You're here before I leave. Me and Daddy—my Lord, Lurleen! You look a mess!"

I drop my head, look at my coat. It looks just like always, to me. My dress is stained, but Johnny can't see that. "What?" I ask.

"You're white as a lily. You must be exhausted." He puts an arm around my waist, takes my hand and leads me inside. "Lyle Gregory was hard on you?"

"Fairly rough. I'll be okay, after I sit a spell."

Johnny helps me out of my coat, and his eyes grow big when he sees my bloody dress. "That looks a sight more than 'fairly rough,' to me. Lyle going to make it?"

"He'll live. Reckon he won't get drunk and ride horseback for a while." I lower my sore bones into the rocking chair by the fire.

Johnny hangs up my coat, goes to the kitchen and returns with a cup of hot water sweetened with honey. "Sip on this while you rest. It'll warm you up a tad." He pulls the quilt from the back of the rocker, and he lays it across my lap.

I smile and thank him, then I remember what he started to tell me. "Say you're going to your daddy's?"

"I'm going to get him, yes. We're going to ride out to see the men at the National Park Service. We're going to tell them no." He smiles, and it's the proud kind of smile I can tell he wants me to mirror. "Lyle might be a drunken fool, but he was right about one thing. Our daddies and granddaddies and great-granddaddies have all lived on this land, and one of these days, I'll have me a son who'll live on this land, too."

My free hand finds my belly before I can stop it, and Johnny sees, cocks his head to one side.

He kneels by the rocking chair. "Lurleen, I know you had your sights set on Nashville, on a house in town and university learning." He holds my hand. "That ain't no kind of life for a country man like me. I need to farm and raise cattle. I have to hunt these here woods and build cabins for newlyweds. This is all I know, Lurleen. Besides, there ain't no better place in the world to raise a family, and it's about time for us to get started on one."

I'm too tired to cry. It wouldn't do no good, no how. I try my best to smile, and I must do okay, because Johnny grins and kisses me full on the mouth, then jumps up and grabs his coat.

"It'll be nigh dark before I'm home. You get some rest, and I'll see you 'round suppertime."

I fall into fitful slumber, dream of Violet wading into the river, of Miss Hazel tying Lyle's bloody leg to the bundle she threw into the waterfall, of Johnny planting corn, of Momma's dirty feet. I'm in a sweat when I wake, and the blood on my dress scares me. Then the world rights itself, and the room comes back to me. I'm going to have to live in Cades Cove until the end of my time, and then I'm going to die in it. The best thing I can think to do is make the time in between living here and dying here as short as I can.

I stand and pull off the ruined dress, throw it on the fire. I don't want rags with Lyle's bloodstains marking this day.

In the bedroom, I hang Johnny's long johns on the bedstead to air, and I pull on another loose dress. Before I know it, I'm wearing my coat, and I'm standing by the porch, hefting smooth river rocks in my hands. Two at a time, I load them into the pockets of my dress and coat, feel them thump hard and heavy against my legs and knees as I walk toward the river.

It's hard to climb the hill toward Abrams Falls weighted down like I am, but I imagine seeing Violet again, telling her how sorry I am, and she will say it's okay. She'll say I'm with her now, where I belong. I think of seeing Momma and Daddy standing on either side of her in heaven, of how they'll open their arms to receive me, and I keep on going.

When I reach the riverbank at the head of the falls, my legs are ready to give out. I sit for a bit, look out at the place where Violet waded into the water. In my mind, she is before me, moving slow and steady, water climbing to her knees, her waist, her neck. Did she know I watched her from the trees? Was she waiting for me to come to her rescue, save her?

Foolish thoughts. She couldn't have known I followed her.

When I saw her loading her pockets with rocks, loping up the path toward the river, I knew what she was up to. That's when I should have said something, took her by the hand, dragged her home. Instead, I watched.

She'd cried every day for thirteen days. Not just now and then, but all the time. Her hollow eyes were bruised like she'd been hit. At first, I'd hold her, rock her in my arms like I did when we was little. Then after several days, I got mad at her. Told her to clean herself up, fix dinner for Walter, come back to the land of the living. When she started to stink, I bathed her in a washtub by the fire. She just sat there, her tears steady streaming, not moving a muscle to help me. The day she quit crying was the worst. I'd ask her a question, and she'd look beyond me, like I wasn't even there. She was gone somewhere inside herself, somewhere only she alone could go. It spooked me.

The night before she walked to the river, as I tucked her into bed, I saw a flicker of my sister behind those blank eyes. It was as if she peered out at me from the darkness of a deep, dank well from which she didn't want to emerge; rather, she wanted me to jump in with her, sink straight to the bottom of the shaft into the soft, swallowing silt.

For a magical, morbid moment, I entertained joining her.

It takes me a couple of tries to stand up now—I'm un-balanced by the load I carry—but I get my feet beneath me. I follow in Violet's footsteps, walk towards the river, and my breath catches as I step into the icy water. It's so cold it feels like it's cutting me, but the mineral scent of river water smells like home to me. I keep going, step towards the rushing current, and the freezing river slides between my calves, my thighs, rises around my waist. The rocks in my dress and coat hold me steady as water sluices around my belly, around the baby that's inside of me. *Can my baby feel the cold?*

The few times after the birthing when I could coax Violet to talk, she'd only say she missed her baby. She'd touch low on her belly, the soft, empty place once filled with something not quite alive, yet still growing. The horrid thing that's out here where I stand. My foot finds something slimy, and I shudder.

Terror rises in me, and I turn to run towards the river-bank, to escape this briny water where dead things float beneath the surface, where the thing that's not quite a baby lies wrapped in a blanket my sister knitted, where she herself now lies bloated and purple. My mouth opens wide, and a scream tries to climb out of my throat, but I'm too cold, too frightened to make a sound. My belly tightens, and I imagine my baby inside, curling and huddling against the icy river.

I'm thigh-deep when I slip on a slick stone, fall face-first, my mouth filling with frigid water. My hands find the river bottom, and silt oozes between my fingers. My eyes are open in the murkiness, and bubbles rise in front of my face as I struggle to stand. I rise to my knees and cough out the scream that finally surfaces.

I claw and stumble my way back to the riverbank, shoulder out of the rock-laden, heavy, wet coat and fall to the ground. I curl into a ball, make myself small, shivering as much from the horror of what I've almost done as from the icy wetness. The sob inside me breaks loose, and I empty out all that I have carried.

Hours later, I stand before the hot stove, stirring venison soup, and Johnny flings open the door.

"I'm home. Sure smells good in here," he calls out before he even sees me.

I want to run to him, but my feet have roots that won't let me move. I squeeze my eyes shut, try to remember how I want to begin. I jump when Johnny touches me.

"Why you cooking with a blanket around your shoulders? You chilled again?" He touches his hand to my forehead. "You're fevered. Come sit down." He guides me toward the rocking chair by my shoulders, and I let him.

"I ain't got the fever. My forehead's hot 'cause I been standing over a boiling pot." I sit in the rocker, and he stands over me, his face full of questions.

"What's the blanket for, then?"

Things ain't unfolding the way I pictured. He's scattering my thoughts out of order. "I got wet. I—I felt in the river."

"Lurleen! That water is like ice. You could catch your death of cold."

He stoops and rubs my arms up and down, and they feel loose, and I know if I shook them, they'd fall to the floor. I could come apart, arms first, then my head, pieces of me scattering across the floorboards.

But I can't do that. I have baby in me. I'm a momma now, and I have to save my baby, even if I didn't save Violet. I have to save my child, the way Momma saved me.

I watch Johnny lay another log on the fire, watch the sparks float upward, light the dark with their tiny glow. "Johnny," I say, remembering the lines I practiced, and he turns to me. "I am glad about the land. I'll live here with you for as long as you will have me."

He scoops me up as though I am a kitten, sits in the rocker with me on his lap. He kisses my forehead. "I will have you forever," he says.

I pull my hand from beneath the blanket and stroke his cheek, look into the pools of his eyes. "You promise?"

He tilts his head. "Course I promise. I promised that on the day we wed, and I ain't a-going back on it. Sickness and health. For better or for worse. I vowed before God."

I press my cheek against his neck, close my eyes. I think I could sleep, then I remember the soup. I move to get up.

"Where you going?"

"Dinner," I say. "Come and eat." I untangle myself from Johnny's arms, from the blanket, and he follows me to the kitchen, pulls out his chair, while I ladle the soup.

I thought I was doing the right thing by letting Violet go, but my thinking was so very wrong. There is no way I can imagine forgiving myself, since even walking into a watery grave couldn't bring me peace. But maybe I can, at least, find Johnny's mercy.

He takes my hands and blesses the food, and when he starts to let go, I keep holding on. "For better or for worse?"

He leans forward, studies my face. "For better or for worse."

I grip his hands tighter, soak up their warmth, feel their roughness beneath my fingertips. "Johnny," I say, "there's some things I've got to tell you."

Kicking Time

The truck sputtered and ran out of gas just as Benjamin pulled into his empty driveway. He headed into the house, his hand pulsating with pain, and he sank heavy onto the plaid sofa. His head pinged like an overfilled basketball as he tossed back two of the pain pills he'd received an hour ago from the hospital pharmacist. He swallowed the pills dry, leaned forward on the couch, and peered into the kitchen at the clock on the wall. Rose should've been home by now—if she was coming home.

"Rose," he said to the empty room, her name thick on his tongue. He'd thought her name fit her perfectly the moment he'd met her; a real American beauty with flushed cheeks, fair skin, and hair the shiny color of newly mined coal. Now early gray streaked her hair, her scarred and pocked face appeared yellowed, and when she'd stabbed a fork deeply into his hand late last night, he knew he'd found her thorns.

He lay back on the couch, but the throbbing in his broken hand prevented sleep. He scratched around the edge of the cast until he popped the skin, and a droplet of blood spread on the frayed cuff of his shirt, a bright red spot on light blue, right next to his embroidered initials. It didn't matter; the ER nurse had ruined the shirt, slit the sleeve up to his elbow, and it flopped around the cast like a broken wing. He closed his eyes. Somewhere in the mist floated Rose's concerned face, Rose's pouting lips, Rose's voice pleading with him as he held the needle over her blue-green vein that first time three years ago. *Are you sure, Ben? Will it hurt? What if I die?*

The metallic sound of a key in the door lock jerked Ben upright. The door swung open, and a gust of wintery air whooshed in around Rose. She stomped snow from her sneakers, looked at Ben's hand, and frowned.

"A cast? Really?" Rose pulled a pack of cigarettes from her purse, then slung it onto a chair. She walked toward Ben, but stopped a few feet away, out of arm's reach.

He blinked a few times to clear the fog of his pain medication. "Really."

"I broke it?"

Ben nodded. "Torn tendons and broken metacarpals." He licked his dry lips, but his parched tongue was like sandpaper on wood. "I need a drink." He shoved himself to a sitting position and massaged his stiff neck with his good hand. Rose rounded the corner, heading toward the kitchen sink. "Whiskey," he said.

"Now you're talking." Plastic jugs bumped against one another as Rose cleared a spot on the kitchen counter, and then the cupboard door thumped and glasses clinked. Rose returned cradling a bottle of Ancient Age in the crook of her arm, two filmy rocks glasses in one hand, her cigarette in the other. She sat on the far end of the couch, overfilled both glasses, and shoved one toward Ben. "Guess you want an apology."

He didn't look at her. Instead, he stared at the bookshelf across the room. Over a hundred volumes of literature and poetry, once neatly alphabetized by author, now lay askew, some with spines turned inward, all covered in gray dust. His gaze settled on the still-intact, leather-bound Shakespeare collection, a graduation gift from his mother.

"What's in a name?" he quoted. "That which we call a rose, by any other name would smell as sweet." He downed the whiskey and set the glass in front of her, motioned for a refill.

Sadness pulled at Rose's mouth, and silence settled between them like evening dew, cold and expected. After a minute, she filled Ben's glass again, topped off hers, then spoke quietly. "Been a long time since you recited poetry to me."

Ben swirled the brown liquid in his glass, but didn't speak.

"You miss it?" she asked.

"What? Shakespeare?"

"Writing poetry. Teaching. All of it. I know you miss it, Benny." She stared at her hands, nibbled at a hangnail. "I miss it, too." She slid a little closer to Ben. "Sorry things turned out like this."

Ben shut his eyes tightly, her apology causing more pain than any broken bone ever could. He searched his mind for the first love poem he'd written for her, back when she was his student during his first year of teaching, but the words and phrases wouldn't line up. If only he could remember, if he could put things in the right order, if he could recite the poem, recite the *I'm sorrys* long past due, then maybe—

He opened his eyes when the weight of Rose's arm pressed into his outstretched leg. She leaned across him and reached to pick up the two prescription bottles on the coffee table. "What'd they give you?" She read the label and let out a soft whistle. "Potent stuff." She unscrewed the top and shook two of the big capsules into her hand, downed them with a gulp of liquor.

"I don't recall you asking to share."

Rose wiped her mouth on the back of her hand, reopened the pill bottle and shook out two more. She opened her hand, lifted her palm to Ben's lips. He eyed her distrustfully, and when she smiled, he leaned forward and opened his mouth, letting her feed his pain. "Bottom's up," she said, clinking her glass against his, and they again drank.

Ben sank against the back of the couch, and Rose scooted closer, settled beside him and sipped from her glass. She traced a finger along the inner seam of his jeans, stopped just short of his crotch. "You just, you know . . . pushed my button. I ain't a whore. No matter *what* your mother says."

She rested her hand on his thigh, and he noticed her fingernails were chewed to nubs, the skin around them red and dry. The clock over the kitchen sink ticked away seconds in the background, and Ben tried to count them, but gave up around six or seven. "I'm out of money, Rose. Truck's out of gas, no food in the house. We gotta do something."

"Something, all right. But not *that*."

"It was a stupid thing to say. I shouldn't have said it. I was. . ."

Rose's jaw flexed and her teeth clenched together so tightly Ben heard them grind like sandstone rocks. "You need a fix." He let out a long breath. "I need a fix. Hand hurts like hell."

She reached for the prescription bottle, opened it, shook out another pill. "Here," she said, shoving the capsule toward his mouth. "This'll take the edge off till I can get us something."

Ben swallowed the pill, washed it down with another swig of whiskey. "Where you gonna get it?" he said, his words already slurring.

Rose again filled Ben's glass and tossed back the last of the Ancient Age straight from the bottle. She looked at him, more stoic than he'd seen her in a long time. "I got an idea. Don't you worry." She stood and took her scarred leather purse from the chair, slung it over her shoulder. "Get some rest."

He closed his eyes, and he thought he heard her whisper. *I'm sorry, Benny. Really.* He must have waited too long to respond, because when he opened his eyes, she was across the room, car keys in her hand. Maybe he'd dreamed those words.

Ben must have slept after Rose left, because when he opened his eyes, the living room had grown dark. He turned on a lamp, stood, and stretched out the kinks in his body. He itched all over.

In the kitchen, he checked the liquor cabinet beneath the counter, but only a half-empty bottle of peach schnapps remained, left over from a Christmas party years ago. He hated peach schnapps. He slammed the cabinet door and checked the time on the kitchen clock. Thirteen hours and twenty-six minutes since his last fix. The longest he'd been without meth in months. He dug at a scab on his shoulder, grabbed the bottle from beneath the cabinet, downed the schnapps, and shuddered.

Our mouths crave juice of summer's peaches. . .

The line from his love poem came back to Ben, too late to recite it to Rose, but it thrilled him all the same. What came next? He scratched his head, his cheek, his neck. Rose would remember. She always memorized his poems, but it would mean more if he could recite it to her, instead of her to him. If he apologized to her, instead of her always apologizing to him. Didn't his remorse always come out flat, worthless? How could he ever ask forgiveness for everything he'd done to her? To his mother? To his father?

Ben walked to the bookshelf, traced his fingertip through the dust, avoiding the books with their spines turned inward, the ones his father had given him before. . .

It was an accident, Mom. I'm so, so sorry.

He'd never said those words to her four years ago, didn't believe at the time he should have to say them. He hadn't wanted to drive, anyway. Plenty of people told his mother, told the police, told the doctors at the hospital before Ben had regained consciousness that he'd pleaded with his father for neither of them to drive. The Hokie game had gone into overtime, and they'd drunk too much, both of them. The serpentine highway between Blacksburg and Bluefield was risky during the best of conditions, but on a snowy night in below-freezing temperatures, it was treacherous.

"I should have stood up to you," he muttered now to the empty room. Even as he said them, the words sounded false. No one stood up to the mayor. No one ever told the man no.

Ben picked up the photo taken of Rose and him during their honeymoon cruise, blew the dust from it and wiped it with his sleeve. God, she was beautiful then. He peered closely, angling the picture to see better in the dim lamplight. When the glass reflected his own image, his breath caught. He looked so much like his father now it always shocked him to see his own reflection. How could he ever look at his mother, apologize to her, wearing the face of the father he'd killed?

Fresh snow flurried around Rose's face as she walked up the slush-covered sidewalk toward Ben's boyhood home. She stood outside the door a moment before ringing the bell, disgust swirling inside her like the dry snowflakes eddying in the wind at her feet. Rose despised his mother. She hated that she stood between tall white columns on the woman's broad porch, hated that it had come to this. Martha Wilson had kept Rose and Ben from having the white-dress church wedding of Rose's dreams, doing everything in her power to break up their relationship. And she'd nearly succeeded, until Ben had finally had enough, had driven

Rose across the state line to Pearisburg, where they'd married in a judge's office. Martha had never forgiven Rose for taking away her only son, and when Rose learned she couldn't bear children, Martha called it God's good justice.

Rose spent the first seventeen years of her marriage trying to prove to Martha—to everyone—that despite what Martha called her "holler-trash upbringing," she was worthy of Professor Benjamin Wilson, the mayor's only son. Even after Rose's father got his settlement money and they could afford nice things, Rose's efforts failed—Martha told her she was trying too hard to fit in.

While standing at her husband's hospital bedside, Rose learned from a nurse that the mayor had died in surgery. She decided right then that the only person she needed to prove anything to was Ben. Four days after the fatal accident, Ben regained consciousness, and he was devastated to learn his mother had held his father's funeral services the day before.

"One day?" he'd yelled at her. "You couldn't wait one more day?" They'd argued so bitterly that hospital security intervened. When Ben refused to speak again to the woman, Rose decided God's good scales of justice had indeed balanced.

After another eight days of hospitalization and a month of physical therapy, Ben came home. He drank even more, took plenty of pain pills, and when Martha's precious boy finally turned to meth, Rose held his hand. A good woman helps her man numb his pain; hadn't her mother taught her that?

Rose now thought of a similar winter; the winter her father lost his leg in a mining accident. The UMWA made sure he received disability, early pension, and a six-figure lump to boot, but it took more than money to satisfy a man made for working. Sedentary, he'd grown more angry and hateful by the day.

Soon after, Rose's mother brought home a brown paper
bag she carried in both hands. In it was a quart jar of
moonshine she'd bought from her shift supervisor at the
Maidenform plant. Rose's father may have been mean
sober, but he was a happy drunk, and even when the trade
of mason jars for money increased to two, three, then four
times a week, her father's bliss remained. Yes, Rose knew
well how to help a man survive his pain.

Now she pressed the doorbell below the historic-register
plaque, listened to the low chimes sound throughout the
two-story colonial.

Martha swung open the door right away, catching Rose
off guard. "What? You think I didn't hear that rattle-trap
pull into the driveway?" Martha jerked her head toward
Rose's faded Trans-Am. "What do you want?"

"Can I come in?" Rose shifted her weight from one
freezing foot to the other, wishing she'd worn boots instead
of her old canvas tennis shoes, now wet with slush.

Martha's eyes roved Rose's body from head to toe, and
she scowled. "What is it you want?"

"Good God, Martha, where are your manners? I come
to tell you Ben's hurt." Rose stood straighter when she saw
Martha's arrogant expression fall.

The woman stepped back and allowed Rose to enter.
Inside, the warm air was delicately scented with the
fragrance of Martha's signature cologne, the honeysuckle
perfume she'd worn since long before Rose had met her
twenty-some years earlier.

"What happened to Ben?"

"Crushed his hand. He's—he's at home, now."

Martha still stood in the foyer, blocking Rose from
entering the formal living room. She propped her hands
on her hips. "How did he do that?"

Rose chewed her lip. *Think.* The image of her father's
leg pinned between two coal cars in the mine returned to

her. "He hurt it. At work." She pointed to the back of her own hand. "Broke some bones here. Ripped up the tendons. It's a real mess."

Martha's over-powdered forehead creased. "Since when does Ben work?"

"He works! We both work." She huffed and looked over Martha's shoulder at the spotless living room, the large crystal art pieces decorating the mantle, dustless dust-collectors she could sell to score the fix she needed. "He got a job at the Celanese plant."

Martha crossed her arms. "In Narrows? That's a long way to drive." Her voice softened. "Especially in winter." She looked toward the window at the ribbon of dark road growing paler under a light coat of snowfall, and Rose knew the woman envisioned the accident years earlier.

"Not like he can get a job in this town." Rose pressed her lips together. Ben had studied hard, worked hard, published, earned his position without relying on his father's status. One drunken mistake in this small town full of smaller-minded people, and everything dissolved.

Martha walked toward the window and stared out at the snow that fell heavier now. She looked frail in her bitterness, hard and brittle.

"Does it make you happy, Martha?"

The woman glanced sharply at her, then turned back to the window, pulling her sweater tightly around her. "Does *what* make me happy?"

"Blaming Ben for Thomas's death."

It surprised Rose to see the blood drain from the woman's face. She reached a hand toward Martha, afraid she would crumble. The woman stared at Rose's extended hand, its welted scratches and chewed nails, and Rose jerked it back, tucked it inside the sleeve of her hoodie.

Martha cringed, then composed herself and squared her delicate shoulders. "I don't blame Benjamin. I never have."

Her voice dropped to a whisper. "Ben must forgive himself."
Then her mouth formed a hard line. "That might be easier
for him, if you hadn't got him hooked on drugs."

Martha turned away again, and Rose caught the motion
of the woman wiping her eyes. Rose opened her mouth to
apologize—wasn't she always apologizing to Martha and
Martha's son?—but Martha spoke first.

"Why are you here? What do you want?" Martha
looked tired now, her gaze cold.

Rose's arms itched, but she dared not scratch in front
of Martha, dared not let her think she'd been using again.
She swallowed, wished she had another drink of whiskey
to wet her dry throat. "Ben needs medicine. We just—we
don't have money for it." Rose rocked side to side, the
effort to stand still more than she could bear.

"You said he got hurt at work."

"He did," Rose said.

"Then workers' comp will pay for his prescriptions."
Martha fingered the pearls at her throat.

Rose worked her aching jaw. She was desperate for a
fix. She looked again toward the crystal on the mantle,
wondered how difficult it would be to melt it. Do you melt
crystal? It was heavy, she knew. Worth its weight in . . . in
what? *Worth its weight.* She'd heard that phrase before,
hadn't she? A poem Ben had read aloud in class one day?

"They will. I mean, comp will pay him back. And then
we'll pay you back. We have to file a claim. It takes time.
But he's hurting *now*, Martha."

"And the drugs you got him hooked on? Is he so far
gone they no longer numb his pain?"

Roses mouth curled into a snarl, and she forced her lips
into a smile. "They do drug tests at Celanese. He wouldn't
be working if he was using, wouldn't have gotten hurt."
She held up her hand in front of the woman's face. "Crushed
the bones. Ripped the tendons. Can you imagine? Whole

thing is in a cast. He'll need all kinds of therapy." Rose shook her head. "He's really bad off."

The woman's gaze softened, but mistrust remained etched in her face. "How much do you need?"

Ben was holding his cramping stomach and pacing the floor when Rose returned near midnight. "Where the hell have you been!" He picked up an empty bleach jug and flung it her direction, where it thumped and bounced harmlessly off the wall.

"Look, it took a while, okay? Stuff don't grow on trees." She held a worn-out, brown paper lunch bag toward him. "Here."

Ben snatched the bag from her and held up his cast, now blood-tinged at one edge where he'd scratched away the skin. "I ought to backhand you."

"Don't you dare," she said.

He hustled toward the couch and held the bag upside-down over the coffee table, shaking it until the small plastic bags fell out across the table. "My god," he said, realizing the words were true. "Where'd you get all this?"

Rose's gaunt face looked smug. "Martha's little vineyard." She laughed at her own joke.

"You went to Mom's? How did you—"

"Don't worry. She thinks you got hurt at work. Celanese plant over in Narrows. We don't have to pay her back until workers' comp pays you back for the medicine."

Rose opened her mouth wide and laughed again, a dry, sucking sound, and Ben noticed how some of her back teeth were starting to blacken. His own were turning darker yellow.

His good hand trembled as he picked up a baggie the size of a piece of chewing gum, and he held it in front of his eyes. His mouth watered, and his teeth chattered, almost in time with the ticking clock in the kitchen.

"Poor baby," Rose said, walking around the coffee table to sit beside him on the couch. "You need help." She fished in the pocket of her hoodie and pulled out car keys, a pipe and a lighter, but Ben stayed her hand.

"No," he said.

She stared at him. "What?" she finally said.

"It's been eighteen hours," he said, peering toward the kitchen clock. "And forty . . . forty-one minutes. Almost nineteen hours."

"I said I'm sorry. It's not like I was out killing time. I was *looking,* Ben. But I'm here now, and I brought plenty of trash."

"What did you say?"

"I said I brought plenty of trash."

"No, about *kicking time.* What'd you say about kicking time?"

Rose wrinkled her nose. "*Killing* time. I said I wasn't out *killing* time." She placed her car keys on the table, reached for a tiny baggie and started to open it.

"No. No." He forced himself not to look at the baggie in her hand, at the crystals he imagined melting, liquefying, so their jagged edges wouldn't cut and slice him as their smoke filled his lungs, their wisps curled through his veins. He turned his face toward the kitchen, where the clock on the wall seemed to tick louder.

"I don't get—don't you want—"

"Mom ask about me?" He turned to search Rose's face. His wife's mouth softened, the way it did right before she lied to keep from hurting him.

"Of course. She knows you're hurt. And she misses her baby boy." Rose fingered the cigarette lighter. "She said you have to forgive yourself. Said it'd be easier if I hadn't got you hooked on drugs." She snorted a harsh laugh.

He pursed his lips, wanted to spit out poison, spit it in his mother's face. She'd taken away his only chance to say goodbye to his father, to say he was sorry. "I hate how she—how she blames you for . . ." he waved his hand, "for all this."

Ben watched as Rose slowly looked around the room, her gaze lingering on the bookshelf, the artwork hanging askew, the dusty antique mirror, the dented bleach jug he'd flung against the wall, as if appraising the dishevelment for the first time. She looked back at him, shrugged and smiled broadly, as if their habit was a joke they shared. It *was* a joke, he knew. He'd dragged her into it. Knew drugs were a way to feed her, make her need him, inject himself into her veins. Now the joke was on him.

He rocked back and forth to the cadence of the ticking clock. "I want to kick. It's been almost nineteen hours. Hear the clock? Almost a whole day. I want to kick. Let's kick, baby."

Slowly she shook her head, a lank of hair falling over one eye. Sometimes when he looked at her, he could almost remember what she looked like when they first met, his American beauty.

"But I bought all this." Her teeth chattered, and she waved a hand over the table. "I got this for us."

Ben's eyes followed the movement of her hand, his gaze settling on the twenty or so tiny baggies—the feast—scattered across the scarred wooden tabletop. Enough to last a few days, if they were careful. He dug around the edge of the cast, scratching until he again brought blood. *You have to forgive yourself.* "I don't want to do this anymore."

Rose hung her head, and when she looked up, Ben was surprised to see her face streaked with tears. Rose never cried.

"Don't, baby." He lifted his broken hand and wiped her cheek with the exposed tips of his fingers. "Don't cry." The ticking clock made his ears itch deep inside. "We can be normal. Be a family, again. You, me, your parents . . . Mom."

"I don't know how to make you happy anymore."

Ben dug at his ear with his good hand. "You always make me happy. Always."

She smiled, sniffed, and opened one of the baggies, shook tiny crystals into the bowl of the green glass pipe, flicked the cigarette lighter, and held the pipe to his lips.

Ben met her red-rimmed eyes, then held up a hand to block the pipe. "Please. Let's at least try."

Rose sat without speaking, her body trembling, and the lighter's flame died between them.

"I want to get better. Don't you want to get better?" He reached out, cupped his good hand over the pipe she held. "We can do this. It's been almost a whole day. We've got a good start."

You have to forgive yourself. Had his mother really said that? His stomach tightened around his need.

He watched Rose's eyes, waited for them to find his, but she looked away, stared at the tiny baggies scattered across the coffee table.

Her tongue darted across her cracked lips. "After this is gone, Benny, we'll kick." She pulled the pipe from beneath his hand, held it to her mouth, and flicked the lighter.

Ben couldn't watch. His mouth watered when he heard her inhale, and he looked away. He stood, and his gaze found the small antique mirror on the wall across the room, the one he avoided each time he walked past. It held a too-familiar face—sometimes full of pity, other times accusing—that he couldn't bear to see. He looked back at the baggies scattered across the table, and lying in their midst were Rose's car keys. He scratched his arm above the cast, swallowed hard as he heard the lighter flick again, and he reached for the keys.

Smoke curled out of Rose's mouth, along with her words. "Where you going?"

He took a step toward the front door, but stopped short when he saw, directly in front of him, his father, dusty and framed in gilt. He swallowed, saw the man's jaw flex. His powerful father. His powerful, alcoholic father.

No. Not his father. His own reflection. *This is me, and I am* not *you.*

He looked back at Rose. "I can't do this anymore."

Her grin said she didn't believe him. "You ain't leaving."

He held out his scratch-welted hand, reached across the meth-scattered table between them. "Come with me. Let's get away from this—this mess. Leave it behind. Start fresh."

Rose flicked the lighter and lifted the pipe to her mouth.

Ben pressed a hand to his cramping stomach, turned away from his wife, closed his eyes, and listened to air whoosh through the pipe. "God forgive me," he whispered. He put his hand on the doorknob. "I'm leaving."

"You'll be back."

Her raucous laughter was patronizing, and its hollow sound followed Ben out the door.

He sat in Rose's Trans Am, letting its engine warm, wondering if he had the guts to pull out of the driveway. He traced his finger over the Firebird's traction control switch, and those words seemed to mean something: *Traction Control.*

Control.

That's what he needed; what he'd never really had. Control.

He'd had no control over driving home from the game, no control over the car when he plunged his drunken father to his death. He had no control over his careening career, over how the whole damn town saw him after that accident. No control over his desperate love for Rose, even as he fed her that first addictive hit.

He pressed a fist against the gripping twist of his stomach. No control over his drug habit.

Until now.

He backed out of the driveway, stomped the gas pedal, and fishtailed onto the snow-covered road. He drove the six miles toward the T—the place where the county road dead-ended against the main highway—without ever seeing another car. At the traffic light where the road ended, he stopped, stared at the red light, then peered in both directions through heavy snowfall. To his left, the road looped back, made a lazy circle that would eventually take him the long way home, back to his Rose, back to those baggies, back to sweet relief, back to hell.

If he turned right, he'd head into the historic district of their small town, head to his mother's house, where maybe he'd find forgiveness, but more likely find judgment: its own kind of hell.

He startled when a horn honked, and he looked in the rearview mirror to see a big, dark pickup truck stopped behind him. Ahead, the traffic light shone a steady green, broken only by the rhythmic swipe of windshield washers pushing away the dime-sized flakes of wet snow.

The horn blared again, longer this time, and Ben glanced into the rearview. He let out the breath he'd been holding and took his foot off the brake. With his one good hand, he gripped the steering wheel until his knuckles turned white—*traction control*—then turned the wheel and drove toward what lay ahead.

Heritage

I've never cared for alcohol. To me, cocktails taste like antifreeze smells, and wine has all the flavor of cough syrup. I wouldn't even have come to the Paxtons' stupid wine tasting if it wasn't an opportunity to be seen by the higher-ups in the Daughters of the American Revolution. It's another rung on the social ladder, one I've been trying hard to climb for years, to make a place for myself and for my daughter, Sarabeth. And yes, I'm pulling my husband Ramsey along with me, whether he likes it or not. We argued about coming, and I won, so he's at the far end of the Paxtons' long, Italian-marble bar, pouting. Ignoring me.

The sommelier from the winery in Beckley works his way toward me, while his burgundy-haired assistant attends the guests at the other end of the bar. I note how her lipstick perfectly matches her hair, and how Ramsey doesn't pay any attention to any of this, but instead, focuses on the wine, holding his glass up to the light before putting it down and jotting a note on his scoresheet.

The sommelier rinses my glass with water from a heavy-looking crystal pitcher, then pours another splash of a different wine and returns the glass to my hand. "I think you'll enjoy this port, Claire," he says. "It has the rich, tart flavor of fresh blackberries, and the infused brandy warms the palate and throat."

I nod and smile. Brandy. Mixed with wine. Sounds like a recipe for disaster.

"This is one of my favorites," says a voice near my ear.

I turn, and it's Beau Paxton. He smells of sea salt and leather, though here in Wytheville, in February, the ocean and beach weather are foolish fantasies. I imagine the money in his family's banks smells just like him.

"Bet you'll like port more than the other reds," Beau says. He's got a smooth, unlined face that's better-looking than my Ramsey's. He was once a handsome quarterback when his high school played ours in the regional finals. Now he's gone to sod around the middle, and his fingers curled around the stem of the wine glass look fat to me, too soft for a man. He tilts his glass toward mine in a toast. "Cheers."

"Cheers," I say, and I like the ringing sound our glasses make when they touch. I sip, and the wine is sweeter than the others we've tasted so far. Richer, too. Mellow. And yes, it is warm in my mouth, warms my throat when I swallow. The smile I feel on my face surprises me. I turn to Beau. "Yes, it's really good."

Marlene Paxton looks at me from the end of the bar, and she graces me with a smile, albeit a small one. Her gravel-gray eyes command deference, even from a distance, so I return her smile, then lower my gaze into the crystal wineglass I hold.

The Paxtons practically own this county, and Marlene is president of the Virginia DAR. Since I haven't been a member a full year, I'm still tiptoeing across proving ground. Nomination for officers will be held soon, and the secretary slot is open this year. It's a long shot, but I want it so badly

I ache for it. Secretary is a servant's role in the Virginia Daughters, but I don't care.

"You like this one, yes?" the sommelier asks. "I knew you would." He pours what's left in the bottle into my glass and Beau's.

"May I see the label?" asks a pan-faced man I don't know from the midpoint of the long bar. There must be fifty people here, maybe more. The sommelier holds up the empty bottle and, as he walks toward the man, he goes into discourse about the port and how it's made. Ramsey, ever the eager student, takes notes.

Beau touches my arm. "Enjoying yourself?"

"Yes," I say, a bit surprised. "You have such a lovely historic home. Ramsey and I have admired it for years. Thank you for having us."

He looks puzzled. "I thought you'd been here before." He glances toward his wife, then back to me. "I'll be honored to give you and Ramsey a tour, if you like." He holds up a hand to wave my husband over, but Ramsey doesn't notice. He turns away. "Ah, well," Beau says. "I'll show you around, and we can show Ramsey later."

I nod and sip from my glass. The port really is good, and a soft *mmm* escapes me.

Beau smiles. "If you like this one, I have a vintage port in my office upstairs that makes it taste like Robitussin."

I giggle, happy to know I'm not the only one here who equates most wine to foul-tasting medicine.

He leans closer to my ear. "Let's tour the house, and you can try it. I don't have enough to share with everyone."

A quick glance around the crowded room confirms that Ramsey is still absorbed in the wine lecture. I stare at him, willing him to look at me, but he asks the sommelier a question, and I know I've lost him. Just behind him, Marlene is schmoozing with the chamber president, and when she laughs at something he says, she throws back her head, exposing her long, perfect throat, ringed with her signature pearls, strung like white teeth.

I turn and follow Beau through the dining room, where he points out a massive, antique English sideboard made of bog oak—wood I've never heard of but plan to look up. I follow Beau down the long, gleaming hallway, then up the stairs. When we reach the landing of the wide, polished staircase, all those sips of wine hit me, and I grab the banister to keep my balance.

"Whoa! You okay there?" Beau catches my elbow in one hand and slides an arm around my waist. "Stairs and high heels don't mix well, do they?"

Heat rises in my face. "No. I'm sorry."

"No apology needed. Shoes like those do amazing things for a woman's legs. Not that yours need any help." He chuckles, and I laugh with him. He waves a hand toward the hallway behind me. "Bedrooms that way, four of them." Then he motions in the other direction. "Two master suites, one here, and one here. The largest is ours, of course." He lays a hand on the heavy-looking door in front of us. "This is my office."

Some tour, I think.

He pulls out a large key and unlocks his sturdy door. "Shame to lock a home office, isn't it? Marlene once hired a catering service, and after the party, we discovered some of her jewelry missing." His lips twist to one side. "Live and learn." He ushers me into his office, and I tell myself it's not the least bit strange when he closes the door behind us.

Beau's gleaming office smells of lemon oil and sweet tobacco. A huge portrait of his father hangs on the wall behind the massive desk, the man an older, grayer, still-handsome version of Beau himself.

Beau motions toward two chairs arranged in front of floor-to-ceiling bookshelves in the corner where a tall, Tiffany-style lamp casts a warm glow over the seats. As he strides toward a small, backlit bar, I feel a true, throat-tightening pang of envy. I've always wanted a house like this—antique artwork arranged just so on papered walls, leather-bound literature perched on polished bookshelves, signs of old money and class everywhere. Marlene's house. I sigh and sit on the edge of a hard leather chair that looks more comfortable than it feels.

"How's Sarabeth's college search coming along?" Beau asks. "Has she heard back from anyone?"

"No word yet." I hold up both hands with fingers crossed, and he nods.

"Kaitlin hasn't heard anything, either, though that doesn't stop her from practically stalking the mailman each afternoon." He holds up a crystal highball glass that sparkles in the buttery light. "Sorry, Claire. I only have whiskey glasses in here. Hope you don't mind." He turns away without waiting for my reply, opens a low cabinet door, and pulls out a squat, black bottle, holds it up, admires it. "Forty-one-year-old tawny. A red blend from Portugal."

His smile is indulgent, as though I'm a child, and I realize I feel like one, and this feels like Christmas Eve. I must be drunk.

"I uncorked it this morning to let it breathe. My mouth has been watering for a taste all day."

As he pours the wine, I scan the titles of the books on the shelves, ponder the miniature pewter Revolutionary soldiers atop a carved wooden relief map on a table in the opposite corner of the room. Marlene is so lucky to have married into this wealth. Not that her parents didn't have money—hers was a fine middle-class family and she lacked for nothing in school—but she didn't come from *Paxton* money. Of course, that doesn't stop her from acting like she made this fortune herself.

He catches me staring. "Your office is nice," I say. *Nice?* "Masculine, I mean." *Really, Claire?* "In a good way."

Beau stares at me, his expression sincere. "Thank you." He looks around, as if seeing the room anew. "Masculine. I like that, yes. Thank you."

He turns back to the wine, and I try to think of something to say. "Kaitlin tells me she's applied to all the Ivy Leagues. I'm sure you are so proud of her."

Beau glances at me, then fills the second glass. "She's a bright young lady." He pauses. "To be honest, I'd be happier if she'd follow in her daddy's and granddaddy's footsteps, be a Cavalier, study finance. Especially since Beau Junior went into medicine and dismissed the family business." His voice bears a hint of bitterness at this last, the first fine crack I've seen in the perfect world of the Paxtons. He steps toward me, offers me a half-full highball. "Then Kaitlin would be closer to home, where I can keep an eye on her."

"I understand. My Sarabeth applied to University of North Carolina and University of Florida. She seems determined to move away, but wouldn't it be wonderful if they could attend UVA together? Especially since they're just becoming close friends." I reach up and accept the glass with a smile, remembering to sniff the blood-colored wine.

"To blossoming relationships," Beau says, extending his glass toward mine. He stands over me, so close his legs brush my knees.

"To blossoming relationships." We sip, *savor*, really, and I almost hate to swallow the rich, velvety liquid. "Oh, Beau," I say, "this is spectacular." I smile and put the glass to my lips, inhaling through my nose as I take another sip.

"Spectacular," he echoes. "Excellent choice of words." He holds his glass to the light, where the crystal facets sparkle and shine through the dark liquid. "Thank you for sharing this with me."

I look up at him, and my thoughts freeze for a second. "But you're sharing it with *me*."

He laughs and holds up his glass. "Truly great things are better when shared, and I'm certain this wouldn't taste nearly so—*spectacular*—if I were drinking it with anyone else." He holds out his hand, and I start to offer him the glass I hold. He reaches into my lap, takes my empty hand and helps me up.

We're merely inches apart. I'm dizzy from standing too quickly, or from the wine, or from both. Beau lifts my hand to his mouth, brushes his lips softly against it. I lean back, but the chair is against me. I've nowhere to go. "Beau," I say.

"How about a refill?" He suddenly turns, leaves me standing there, my hand still posed awkwardly in the air. What just happened? I wince and drop my head. He was just being an elegant host, wasn't he? It's the way the upper crust behaves.

I look at the glass in my hand, unsure of what to do, so I quickly down the rest of the port, blot the wine from my lips with the back of my hand, and smooth my dress. I feel anything but composed.

"We should probably get back to the party," I say, wishing Ramsey were by my side so I could take his hand, tickle his palm, our secret signal for *Get me out of here*. I step toward Beau.

"Your turn," he says.

"Excuse me?"

"Your turn to make a toast."

"Oh. Ah, let me see." I try to think of something witty. "I don't usually make toasts. Let me think a moment." I straighten my spine, lift my chin, and hold up my glass, certain this posture will cause brilliance to flow from my lips.

It doesn't work. The room is getting hot. I glance around, desperate for inspiration. My gaze falls on the miniature soldiers. "Oh! To the Daughters of the American Revolution!" I lift my glass.

Beau tries to stifle a snicker but fails. He bursts into laughter, and after an instant of feeling offended, I join him. Tears puddle in his eyes, and soon we're both lost in a fit of giggles.

"To the D-A-R!" Beau shouts, holding his glass toward the ceiling. We both crack up again, and soon my eyes are tearing.

"To revolution!" I say. We laugh until I feel lightheaded and breathless, and in the process of trying to compose myself, I spill droplets of wine on the front of my dress. "Oh!" I touch the spot with my fingers, and Beau quickly pulls out his handkerchief and dabs at the wetness. I start to take the handkerchief from him, and when I look up Beau's mouth is nearly touching mine.

I gasp before he kisses me.

When his mouth leaves mine, I find myself leaning against him, and he's supported by the edge of his desk. I'm standing between his legs. "No!" I put my hand to my mouth. I turn, but Beau grabs me by the shoulders, holds me steady.

"Careful," he says, and I realize I've almost fallen.

"I didn't want—I can't—we shouldn't do—"

"Shhhh." Beau's smile is both sad and tender when he presses a finger to my lips, and he caresses my cheek with the back of his hand. "I didn't mean to upset you, Claire. Please accept my apologies." His face tilts to one side, and in the golden light, his eyes are kind and understanding, and he's again that handsome football star from high school, the boy who all the girls wanted. "I simply . . . well, I haven't felt this kind of thrill in a long time," he says. "Is it really so wrong to give in to a brief moment of happiness? One small moment in time?"

I feel sorry for him, this man who has everything. I turn away from his eyes and the look in them that makes me want to tell him *I'm* sorry, the look that makes me want to comfort him, hold him. There's a photo of Marlene on his desk. Her hair is upswept, her smile is brilliantly white, and there's a double strand of graduated pearls gracing her delicate collarbone. Marlene is beautiful. She gives her daughter everything I can never give mine. She has everything I've never had. Everything I want. She has this wealthy man who stands in front of me, this man who kissed me. This man who, at this one instant in time, wants me more than he wants her.

I close my eyes, and from down below us comes the sound of laughter, then of music. I rise on my tiptoes, lean into Beau.

Every day since my indiscretion five weeks ago, a little bit more of me fades away. Someone once told me that words carry more weight than stones, but mine are as flimsy as feathers, floating over the heads of the people I'm talking to. Like the words I say to Sarabeth, who no longer listens. My actions, though, the things I do and the things I've done, those hold the weight of the world.

"Don't think I won't take that phone away from you, Sarabeth. Look at me when I'm talking to you." I wipe my hands on a plaid dishtowel. "In my day—"

"In *your day*. You always talk about your day, but this isn't your day, it's *my* day. And in *my* day, we text when we—"

"Sarabeth Cresdollar! You will not speak to me like that. Give me that phone. Give it to me!" I grab the cell phone from my daughter's hand, bending back her fingers until the flesh of her palm mottles. That's when I see the writing, the tiny letters and numbers she's penned on her hand. "What is this?"

"It's formulas. For algebra class." Sarabeth blinks hard as her too-long bangs snag on her eyelashes.

"It's cheat notes, that's what it is. You're cheating! Now go wash it off before Marlene gets here."

Tears spring to Sarabeth's eyes as she slides off the barstool, her long skinny legs angling like a praying mantis. "It's notes, Mom! I'm not a cheater!" She runs down the hallway toward the guest bath, and then the door slams.

Why did I do that? I grip the countertop. It's my grandmother in me, her meanness rising to the surface, like the scum on a pond. It's the way she treated Momma and me, lashing out in anger, no matter if we were the cause of it or not. I don't want to be like my grandmother, but I don't want to be like my mother, either: kowtowed and meek, no backbone at all.

Momma wasn't always like that, wasn't always silent and weak. She'd been smart and strong until Daddy left, until her mother did that horrific thing to her. Then she fell into a deep depression, fell hollow and simple. My classmates called her retarded and stupid, said the apple didn't fall far from the tree.

The doorbell chimes. I look at the clock, and it's quarter till. Marlene's early. I smooth my dress, check my hair and my smile in the entryway mirror before opening the door.

"Good morning, Kaitlin. Come on in. Sarabeth's getting her things." I step aside for the dark-haired teen to enter, then I wave toward her blonde-haired mother in the boxy Volvo wagon. "Mornin', Marlene. It's a gorgeous day, isn't it."

Marlene tilts her head out the car window and smiles, her white teeth framed by coral lips. "Just lovely, Claire. See you at the DAR meeting later?"

"Yes, of course." I hate the way my words come out, a bit too high-pitched and bright, and my face burns. "If you'll excuse me, Marlene, I'll see what's keeping Sarabeth. I'm sorry she's taking so long this morning." I shut the door on Marlene's "No worry," and I step past Kaitlin to hurry down the hallway. "Sarabeth?" I push open the bathroom door. "Are you ready?"

Sarabeth arranges the fingertip towel the precise way I've taught her. "Yes."

I yank a tissue from the holder on the countertop. "Here. Your mascara's smudged. For heaven's sake, child, you can't go out of here looking like you've cried, even if you have." I tilt back my daughter's chin, then swipe beneath her lashes. "There." Sarabeth tries to push past me, but I grip her arm and deadpan her. "Be on your best behavior around Marlene and be sure to thank her for giving you a ride."

"I always do." She smirks.

"You mind your manners with her *and* with me, you hear? I worked for three years to wrangle my way into the Virginia Daughters, and just because I'm in doesn't mean you're a given. You'll be up for vote this summer, and if Marlene doesn't want you in, you don't stand a chance. If she sees an ounce of insurrection in your spirit, she'll fence you out, just to spite me." I release the grip on Sarabeth's arm, smooth out the pucker in her sweater, realize I'm acting desperate, like my momma. I try to smile, speak in a pleasant tone. "I don't like arguing with you, Sarabeth. It's just that—well, we have a family history to uphold. Daughters of the American Revolution. Do you understand what that means?" Inwardly, I marvel at her obstinance. What happened to the sweet little girl whose eyes sparkled over the tiniest gesture, over ice cream cones, over new crayons, over bedtime kisses?

"Yeah, revolution means we revolt," Sarabeth says. "That's what it means, Mother. We revolt!" Sarabeth waits until she's halfway down the hallway and out of reach before she turns to glare at me.

I'm not far from her heels, though she keeps moving, the same way I stayed out of reach of my grandmother. It's a shame my momma didn't stay out of my grandmother's grasp. It's a wonder that hateful woman even allowed Momma to birth me, given that she fished out the shrimpling from my momma with a knitting needle after my daddy bolted. My only chance at a sibling, gone. Momma never stood up to her. Her, nor anyone. Momma was an outsider. Someone people pitied.

"There you are!" says Kaitlin when we reach the entry-way, her smile uneasy. She looks at me, then at Sarabeth, picks up on the tension. "You didn't forget your formulas for the algebra practice session, did you?" She holds up her hand. "I wrote mine on my palm, so I could study them all morning."

Sarabeth shoots me another hateful glare and bounds down the front steps. Kaitlin turns her sunlight toward me. "That's a lovely dress, Mrs. Cresdollar."

"Thank you, Kaitlin." It's in me not to trust her, but her expression is genuine enough, so I smile back.

Sarabeth turns on the walkway. "I think it makes you look fat." She spins on her foot, and gravel beneath her shoe scrapes the stepping stone the same way her words scrape my nerves.

"Why, Sarabeth!" Marlene scolds. "That wasn't very nice. I think your mother looks quite stylish this morning."

My teeth grit into a smile, and I shrug. "Teenage girls." I swish my hand in the air and pretend Sarabeth's words don't matter, that Marlene's matter even less. "All those hormones floating around. They can't help their moodiness."

"True," Marlene says as the girls climb into her car. "But they must learn to be polite, even when they don't feel like it, don't you agree?"

I don't know if her sermon is meant for Sarabeth or for me, but I nod and wave and smile as Marlene backs out of the driveway. I shut the door and lean against it. I think I might hate her.

I glimpse myself in the mirror again, and I turn to face it. Okay, I don't want to *be* Marlene. I want to be *better* than her. I want my chance to look down on her and all those other hometown debs, who for so long looked down on me. My hands find my belly. I stand straight and appraise myself surrounded by the mirror's gilt frame. Maybe there's a bit of a paunch there, but I've weighed the same all week, give or take an ounce or two. I decide to change my dress.

I slide hangers across the rack in my closet, searching for a dress I've never worn to a DAR meeting. Marlene will announce nominees for the office of secretary today, and I want to look perfect, just in case. I pick the lilac: a perfect knockoff of the Lilly Pulitzers that Marlene often wears.

If Marlene and her Cabriolet-convertible-driving friends hadn't been so haughty when we were teenagers, hadn't looked down their perfectly shaped noses at me, hadn't acted as if our high school was the set of *Dynasty* or *Falcon Crest* and that I—"the blue-collar baby," Marlene had once called me—didn't belong there, I probably wouldn't have had sex with her husband. "He's not all that, anyhow," I mutter. Without his family money, what would he be? Just a small-town boy like my Ramsey.

Ramsey could have stopped it, couldn't he? If he hadn't pouted, if he'd been more attentive, if he'd noticed me staring a hole in him from the other end of the bar, noticed me leaving the room with Beau . . . but he never even acknowledged I'd been missing when I came back downstairs. I'd attempted to cover the bright-red mixture of pride and shame that burned on my face with a second coat of face powder, and when I took Ramsey's arm, he smiled as if he'd forgotten our tiff, and he said the wine had given me a rosy glow. I couldn't even look at Beau.

Besides, Beau's too wormy for me. Ramsey would say *snaky,* but snakes have more spine. I mean, if I'd have thought for a flashing second that we'd have come to coupling, I'd at least have been prepared with my diaphragm and a gallon of spermicide. Lysol, too, since I've thought of his fat, moist hands since the moment he rolled off me.

Beau had protection in his bottom desk drawer, which says a lot about the way the worm functions in high society.

The box wasn't new, either, because when he shook it, only two square packets fell out. Natural Rubber Latex with Ribs. *This product contains natural rubber latex and may cause allergic reaction. Condoms are intended to prevent pregnancy, HIV/AIDS.* . . .

The packet lay on the floor next to us, and I read its microscopic print while Beau humped and spasmed over me like a dying duck. I should have been worried that the condom might be past its expiration date, but thank God, it held. It wasn't my finest moment.

I push away these thoughts—yet again—and snap a sheet of tissue paper smooth, line two large gift boxes first with the tissue paper, then with waxed paper, so I'll have something nice-looking in which to deliver dessert to the DAR meeting. I think about the importance of presentation; I wonder how well I've prepared Sarabeth for the social pressure of this club she'll hopefully soon enter. Every little thing seems to count far beyond its worth, and I ponder if I'm crazy or just *wrong* to put so much stock in the opinions of Marlene and her minions. I mean, the way she reprimanded Sarabeth this morning! What would she have done if I'd scolded Kaitlin that way?

Just as I start to ice the marbled cupcakes (the only recipe of my mother's that I own), the phone rings. I ignore it, let the answering machine do its job. I still need to pick up the girls before the meeting. I don't have time to chat.

It's Theresa Blevins on the recording. "Would you be a dear and stop by Cora's Florals to pick up the officers' corsages for the meeting? It's on your way, so I trust you'll take care of it. I'll be sure to mention your helpfulness to Marlene this afternoon. See you soon!"

I groan. I press the *Delete* button on the machine and catch my reflection. I look as tired as I feel, and my shoulders are hunched with the weight of all that's on me. I arch my back and hold my head like I'm balancing a stack of books, like they taught us in Home Ec, but I feel my spine compress, bulge under pressure.

In the wee hours this morning, I'd lain awake, agonizing again, shame stealing my sleep. My husband snored softly, and my heart swelled with love and guilt each time he inhaled. Had I really thought sex with a wealthy man could make me more than a blue-collar baby? My grandmother had said many times, *You can't get above your raising, might as well own who you are.*

Ramsey had rolled over then, spooned against me. He draped his arm across me, his hand settling low on my belly, and he let out a satisfied hum near my ear. I buried my face in the pillow to smother my sob.

Now my hands tremble as I rush to box the cupcakes. I load the car and zip down the highway, whip into the florist shop, then dart through traffic to reach the high school on time. I use a tissue to dab the fine sheen of sweat from my forehead as I swing through the school roundabout to pick up the girls. They're blissfully quiet in the backseat, nodding their heads in tandem to whatever is playing on Kaitlin's fancy iPod, each girl plugged into one ear bud. I imagine that if Marlene were driving, she'd probably be holding engaging conversation with the two girls, but I relish their silence. I need time to think.

Three years. Three years I chased down dates and names and family history. So I could belong, so I could fit in with those privileged girls who in school flung snarky comments and snide looks like bricks at me, so I could *show them*, so I could stack those bricks and climb on top of them, so I could be as high—no, *higher*—than them. I traced my family history all the way back to the Boston Tea Party. Back to people who stood their ground, who made a better life for their families. Those people are my lineage. They're Sarabeth's lineage, too. I did it for my daughter, so she'll have a better place in society, a better life, better everything. And now I've done something stupid that might ruin everything, mess it all up not just for me, but for Ramsey, and for our daughter.

Minutes later when I park the car in the VFW lot, Kaitlin pulls out her earbud, leans forward, and places her hand on the seat. "Mrs. Cresdollar, if you'll pop the trunk, I'll carry in the corsages for you."

"Thank you, Kaitlin. That's very sweet of you," I say to her reflection in the rearview. I turn around in time to see Sarabeth smirk at me. The girls open both back doors, but I reach back and catch Sarabeth's hand. "Sarabeth, may I have a word with you?"

She gives me an eye-roll. "Whatever." She pulls her hand away and closes the car door.

Kaitlin steps out, and I pull the trunk-release lever, then turn around in the seat to face Sarabeth. "Do you want to be in the Daughters?"

Her lips part, and she gives me an incredulous stare. "Look, Mom, I'm doing all I can, okay! I'm not going to do anything to embarrass you in front of 'the ladies.'" She makes quotation marks in the air with her fingers, something she knows drives me crazy.

"That's not what I'm talking about." I soften my voice. "You'll never be an embarrassment to me, sweetie." I lean toward her, wedging myself between the front seats, reaching again for her hand. "Do you want this? Is it important to you?" I wave a hand toward the VFW building. "These meetings, The Daughters of the American Revolution . . . does it mean anything to you?"

Sarabeth looks over my shoulder to where I know some of the members are air-kissing Marlene's cheeks at the door before filing into the building. "I know it's important to you. You've worked hard for it." She lowers her voice to a whisper. "And today you're going to get it."

"What? What do you—"

"Marlene is nominating you for secretary today. And like you said, if Marlene nominates someone. . . ."

I should be thrilled, ecstatic that I've proven I'm worthy of being her contemporary—maybe one day even her friend—but I'm half-sick hearing this. Not because of what happened with Beau, but because Sarabeth inadvertently pointed out what I know to be true. This isn't about my daughter at all: it's one hundred percent about me.

I intertwine my fingers with my daughter's. "The ladies," I say, making an air quote with my free hand, and I make myself smile to keep from crying. "Is being one of them important to you?"

Sarabeth shakes her head in a slow, steady motion. "Not really." She stares out the window a moment, her profile part child, part woman.

She turns back to me, and her gaze is soft and wise beyond her years. "I know you've worked hard to be in this . . . this *club*. And I'm proud of our family heritage and all the, you know, the revolutionaries. But you're not like those women in there." She glances over my shoulder. "You're not fake like they are. You're real."

Real? I've cheated on my husband. I've tried for years to be someone I'm not—the greatest lie I could ever tell. I shake my head. "I love you, Sarabeth."

Her eyebrows flicker. "I love you, too, Mom."

Kaitlin pecks on the car window by my seat and shows me the white box of corsages. "Ready?"

"Yes. Go on ahead, dear. We'll be right behind you." I turn back to Sarabeth. "Help me with the cupcakes?"

Sarabeth and I retrieve the cupcakes from the still-open trunk, and I use my elbow to close it. My steps are heavy as I carry the cupcakes toward the VFW entrance, and I step on a stone that rolls beneath my shoe, and I stumble. I catch myself, but I am shaken.

"You okay, Mom?"

I turn and nod at my daughter, but my mouth is too dry to speak.

Marlene smiles as I near where she stands on the portico, and her eyes are molten silver in the sunlight. The double strand of pearls at her throat appears to glow from within, but I see them as a beautiful noose.

"Thank you for the corsages," she says. "Theresa told me you picked them up. I wondered if you would."

"What do you mean?"

Marlene's smile tightens. "You've got a lot going on. You're a busy lady. That's all."

She knows. I wonder if Beau told her right away, or maybe she pulled it out of him. Or perhaps she saw us go upstairs and figured it out on her own.

She appraises the box in my hand. "What's that?"

"Cupcakes. It's my turn to bring something sweet."

She smiles, but her voice comes out hard and flat. "Perfect. It'll feel just like a child's birthday party." She waves a dismissive hand to a low table near the door—*outside* the door. "You can set them over there."

I draw in a slow, deep breath, as if air were strength. "Here." I hand her the box of cupcakes, turn and take the second box from Sarabeth's hand, stack it on top of the one Marlene holds. It is as if I'm handing her millstones—my arms feel floaty with release and relief.

Marlene's perfectly arched eyebrows lift.

"I can't stay," I say. "Hope y'all enjoy these." I realize I'm grinning, enjoying the honey-sweet taste of the word *y'all* coming from my mouth again.

"But Mom," Sarabeth says. "You're being nom—I mean—" She looks at Marlene, immediately drops her gaze to her own feet. Her deference makes me feel ill.

"What are you doing, Claire?" Marlene's stare is stony. "Go inside."

I steadily hold her condescending glare. "No thank you."

"What?" Her face is kinetic, moving like ripples on a pond, changing from frustration, to confusion, to disappointment.

I wave a hand toward the door. "The Daughters . . . this is not for me."

She eyes me warily, and beside me, I feel Sarabeth straighten.

"Well," Marlene says, "you can quit the group, but you'll always be a Daughter." She sniffs. "It's your heritage."

I take my daughter's hand in mine. "Yes, it is." I look at Sarabeth. "It's *our* heritage."

I lean around the cupcake boxes and kiss Marlene's cheek. Not an air kiss, or a cheek-to-cheek brush, but a real kiss, my lips to her cheek for a lasting moment. "Thank you for everything." I glance toward the door, behind which stands the group of women I desperately wanted to belong to, the group that now, finally, wants me.

The smile on my face is so broad I feel it swell and surge through my entire body, and I turn it toward my daughter. "Ready, honey?"

Sarabeth's grin mirrors my own, and it's as if her smile causes my imagination to catch fire and illuminate my future. I will tell Ramsey what I have done. I will beg him to love me, still. We'll follow Sarabeth to school in North Carolina, or Florida, or wherever she goes, and we will start over as a family. We'll create a new heritage for our daughter, our family, a heritage of our very own.

Or the opposite could happen. Ramsey might divorce me. Sarabeth might be ashamed of me. If that happens, I might lose my mind like my mother did.

My heart gallops as I hold my daughter's hand and we walk down the steps, leaving Marlene and The Daughters of the American Revolution behind. Beside me, Sarabeth squeezes my hand. She briefly closes her eyes against the late-day sun. At least for now, she is smiling.

Big Empty

Romie and I haven't talked since we left our West Virginia homeplace over two hours ago, both of us teary-eyed, too afraid to put words into the space already overfull of emotion. Every now and then, I hear Romie sniffle in the seat beside me, and she'll squeeze my knee, or I'll squeeze hers. It's the only way to say what we feel. It surprises me then that she speaks when we're partway through East River Mountain Tunnel.

"Look at them cracks," she says. "You think it's even safe to drive through here?"

I register her words and peer out the Jeep window at the long, zigzagged cracks between the bricks that hold the land away from us. "I feel safe," I say. And I almost do. Five years of underground mining taught me to seek a measure of calm in the disquiet of trespassing in the belly of the earth. There's always danger, sure—men get crushed in roof falls, die in methane fires and explosions, breathe silica and coal dust that seizes up their lungs—but we got to keep the lights on somehow, don't we? Need coal to do that. Still, Romie says it's time everybody admits that tearing apart a mountain can kill you. She says violence done to the land can never come to a good end.

That's why we're leaving.

I reach out a hand and lay it on the soft mound of Romie's belly, as if I can protect this life inside of her that is part mine. She lifts my hand, kisses my palm, and places it again over her womb as we leave the tunnel and drive into morning brightness.

Romie miscarried her first baby. We learned she was pregnant with that one on the day of Daddy's funeral, but we should have suspected it sooner, as Romie had been sick a while. She had it in her head that she had Crohn's disease, like my daddy. I have to admit, I worried about that, too, her not eating much, sick to her stomach, losing weight—just like Daddy started out. Even when she fainted next to Daddy's casket, I never thought *baby*. People faint at funerals, don't they? Grief, stress, exhaustion. Lord knows, she'd worn herself down those last days Daddy was alive, cleaning him, changing him, feeding him ice chips or broth with a teaspoon. She hardly slept.

It was Momma's oldest friend, Bessie Harmon, who held Romie's head in her lap right there on the floor of the funeral home, looked up at me with a smile and said, "You don't know, do you? She's with child." Bessie was known all over Stump Branch to be some kind of seer, but if she knew then that Romie's baby wouldn't live but another four months, she didn't let on.

The doctor said there was no explanation they could find for the late miscarriage, but Romie blamed it on the land. Said the land was poison, poisoned by mountaintop removal mining and the mine owners. Said if we keep on killing the land, the land has no choice but to kill us right back. I can't tell you how it hurt to hear her say those things.

Romie said Daddy felt that way about the land, too. After he died, when she told me about him wanting to blow up the mine where I worked, it shocked me. Made me stop and think. My daddy loved mining. Or used to, before they started lopping off the mountains. Over thirty years he worked underground. Went from shoveling coal into a rail-cart to watching it gouged out with a continuous miner and dumped onto conveyor belts. I seen his face the first time he saw the dragline megaexcavator shearing off the head of Kayton Mountain. Looked like he'd get sick.

Made me feel sickly, too, watching the monster that stands taller than Lady Liberty eat two-hundred-forty ton of mountain in every bite, two bites a minute. *Progress*, they call it. Progress that puts thousands of underground miners like me out of work. Progress that changes the land forever. Progress that pumps sickness into the water supply, kills fish and deer and daddies and babies.

It was Daddy's plan for me and Romie to pack up and head to North Carolina. Romie said we needed to get out of the West Virginia mountains before the coal companies flattened them all, before the mountains buried us in return. I could hardly bear it when Daddy agreed with her. It felt like a message from beyond, then, when we learned on the first anniversary of Daddy's death that Romie was pregnant again. I knew right then that no matter how much I love underground mining, we had to leave.

By the time we drive through Mount Airy, we're breathing easier, talking easier. We plan how to decorate the nursery, and I tell Romie I want to do it in Flintstones. Put a big old Pebbles and a Bam-Bam holding a club on the wall over the crib. Romie looks horrified, and I goose her kneecap, feel a thrill in my chest when she giggles. I'm excited at the chance for a fresh start, but I still feel the cord of the mountains pulling at me every time I look in the rearview mirror. I stare ahead and make myself look towards what will be.

*

Three weeks into my new job, I still ain't used to working in the Greensboro heat. I take off my hard hat, wipe the sweat and yellow dirt from my forehead and look toward the treeline, thirsty for shade. My first gig with the crew at Billings Construction is to build a home improvement warehouse, one of them big-box stores that eats up acres of land. Two of the men I work with are from West Virginia, and the owner Mack Billings used to spend summers with his grandparents up in Fairmont. He took a liking to me right away, said he'd hire more West Virginia boys if they'd come down here. Said we're the best workers he's got, 'cause we know labor, and we know hard times, and we ain't afraid to earn our pay.

I'm earning it, all right. I'm on my second T-shirt today—first one was dripping wet by ten-thirty—and it's not even lunchtime. Leveling footers for concrete under the Carolina sun makes underground mining in the cool darkness seem like a pleasant memory, so I know the heat must be affecting my mind.

Mack landed a contract to build two of the big stores, one each on opposite sides of Greensboro, and he said that'll keep us tied up for nearly a year, though there's a short break in between he'll try to fill. That's security like I've never had. We've got good insurance that even covers our families, so we don't have to worry about paying the hospital when Romie has the baby.

There's other benefits, too. Mack graduated Chapel Hill, and he's all about his men getting an education. He told all of us that if we get our EMT licenses, he'll pay for the classes, plus he'll up our pay seventy-five cents on the hour. Only three months to graduate, so that's a deal I'm taking. Mack said it makes us safer workers, and it lowers company insurance, too.

Romie loves the idea. "I'll study your books alongside you, Jasper," she says, tossing aside another empty cardboard box. She's done most of the unpacking herself while I work, which is just as well, since she's particular about where everything goes. *Nesting,* Mack called it. "If we study together," Romie says, "when the baby's born and I go to nursing school, I'll have a jumpstart on the other students."

I think it's a fine plan, and before long, we're discussing aortas and hemophiliacs at the dinner table.

The whole thing seems funny to me, and I tell Bucky and Mack about it over lunch. Mack runs a hand through his bristle-brush red hair, looks at me with that squint he gets when he ain't sure about something, and he tells me to be careful about letting Romie get smarter than me. I ask him what he means.

"You can't let your woman pass you by, Jasper. Got to stay one step ahead of her. Be smarter, be stronger, keep her under control."

I have to laugh. He don't know Romie like I know Romie. There ain't no keeping that woman under control.

Mack watches me a full minute, then he puts a hand on my shoulder. "Tell you what," he says, "why don't we go to B.G. McGee's on Saturday, grab a burger and a beer, and watch the Tarheels beat the Mountaineers."

"I'll be there," I say. "And we'll drink a cold one and watch the Mountaineers whup the Tarheels."

Saturday rolls around, and I'm surprised at the way Mack's tongue loosens after he downs a few. He starts talking about women, admits he's fresh out of his second marriage by only a few months.

"Married Satan's spawn the first time," Mack says. "The other one wasn't bad, at first, but then she got above me." He lifts an eyebrow, a warning.

"How do you mean?"

He draws the last from his bottle of beer, throws up a meaty hand for the bartender to bring him another. "She was—*is*—an attorney."

I let out a whistle and laugh. "That had to hurt."

Mack laughs, too. "It could have. She was fair, though, seeing as how I put her through law school. You know that mirrored-glass building on Eugene Street? That's her law firm. I built it for her. She took that, I kept the house." He swabs at a puddle of ketchup with a french fry, downs it, then looks at me straight-faced. "Be careful is all I'm saying."

"I'm not sure I understand."

"Romie wants to go to nursing school. You work construction." He lifts his bottle, as if in a toast. "Reputable business, no doubt. It's done me well." He pulls a swig from his beer. "I got a degree in engineering, studied a little business along the way, decided I'd start my own company. Had my degree before she had hers. But while I was working, starting my business, building us a house, throwing up stores and condos and law firms, she was getting smarter. Too good for me. Next thing I know, she's marrying a judge. Someone who understands her, she said, who can relate to her." His voice goes up an octave at this last, and I press my lips together to keep from grinning.

I take a drink and think about Mack's words, then I square my shoulders. Mack don't know us. He don't know what Romie's done for me, for Daddy. He don't know she's the one who took Daddy's OxyContin to Jimbo's house that night and made the trade for the stack of cash that brought us here. She wouldn't let me risk losing my job, said if she got caught, they wouldn't be as hard on a pregnant woman.

Mack's eyebrows raise, and I realize I'm looking at him harder than I mean to. "That won't happen to us," I say. "We've been through a lot together. We're having a baby."

He lifts his beer again, this time towards me, and our bottles ring together. "Congratulations, man. I wish you all the best in the world."

*

Romie and I decide we'll call our baby girl Mariah Jane when she's born, name her after our deceased mothers. I pray each night she'll be born healthy, with my blue eyes and Romie's pout of a mouth. We've been here three months, and Romie spends her days now shopping for miniature dresses, applying to nursing programs, and reading used textbooks so she can get ahead before school starts in the fall. "The baby's going to eat up a lot of my time, Jasper," she says, "so I want to learn all I can while I have some peace and quiet."

I ain't forgot what Mack said, and he'd remind me of it, if I did. I pay attention to what Romie reads and what she says, and I keep some of the books she's read in my truck nowadays. I read history and Hemingway during lunch break, work on my own education, so we can stay on level ground.

It takes no time to finish the first home improvement store, and Mack gets us a contract on a new spread of condominiums on the far end of Wendover. Our second day on the new site, Bucky calls in sick, and Mack points me toward his new Cat 568 Forest Machine. "Looks like you're clearing today."

My jaw drops. I've driven dozers before, but not a forest machine, and I've never cleared land. Mack had let me play on it one day shortly after he bought it, raising and lowering the boom, opening and closing the grapple claw with a joystick that moved as easily as the hand-me-down Atari I'd played with growing up.

Now he spreads the blueprints across the picnic table in front of the small trailer that serves as our portable office, and he jabs a thick finger at the overlapping circles that indicate trees. "All these trees have to go," he says. He shields his eyes from the morning sun and points far left of the trailer, where packed yellow dirt gives way to scrub brush and several acres of loblolly pine. "Start at the far end there. Get as much as you can cleared by lunch, moving back this way."

I smile when I fire up the 568. "Killdozer," Bucky calls it, after some old movie he'd seen where machinery goes wild and kills people. Killdozer rumbles beneath me, and as I shift the gears, raise the boom and swing, my grin grows broader. I throw a thumbs-up Mack's way, and I see him laugh. With an easy flick of my wrist, Killdozer moves forward, not in a lurch like the D9T dozer I sometimes drive, but smooth, like we're rolling on glass, not rocky dirt. "This here's power!" I yell.

In under a minute, I've crossed the expanse of yellow, reached the tree line, and there I bring Killdozer to a rest. I look back over my shoulder, but Mack's moved on to other things, pointing and ordering the crew around the site. I take a deep breath, raise the boom, and open the grapple. I've seen this done before, know how to fell a tree with a boom—start halfway up to keep from getting your head conked—but now it's here in front of me, acres of sweet-smelling timber. It's my hand on the joystick. It's my job.

I think of Daddy and swallow against the knot that comes in my throat. He'd like this sun-colored piece of equipment, like to crawl up in here with me, see how easily Killdozer maneuvers. I manage the controls, simple to do, open the grapple, and the metal claw grabs the first pine midway up the trunk. I startle at how easily the tree shatters, quicker and smoother than snapping my fingers. It's about a seventy-footer, and just like that, it's split in half.

My heart beats faster than I've known it to for a while, and I pick up the top of the tree, swing the boom to the side and start my stack. Back to what's left of the tree, I maneuver the grapple to the base of the pine, snap it off like I'd break a toothpick, one quick and easy motion, lift it to lie alongside the treetop. I glance at my watch. Less than a minute.

I figure sixty trees an hour, give or take. Four hours later, I've cleared at least an acre. When I climb down off Killdozer, my hands tingle from the vibration of the joysticks. I don't want to look behind me, at where I've been, what I've done, but I have to count the stacks, survey the damage.

Standing beside the 568, I feel small, but I shrink to puny when I walk to the last stack of trees I made, see the oaks and maples and pines smashed into splintered haystacks jutting twenty or so feet in the air. I turn away, and my eyes find the bare ground where I've been. Crater-size holes pockmark the dirt where root-bases once sunk deep. Scrub brush lies bent and flattened where Killdozer—and I—left tracks.

I think of the waste back home that once was Kayton Mountain, and my stomach knots up. I close my eyes, try to imagine the condominiums from the drawing on the wall in Mack's office trailer, the playground area with the wooden jungle gym where kids will laugh someday soon. This here's nothing like what's been done to Kayton and hundreds of other mountains where I'm from. This is hardly any harm at all.

A week passes, and on Wednesday night Mack calls me at home to tell me that Bucky has lost his job and gone to jail. Busted selling a bale of weed—I didn't even know marijuana came in bales—so he's making me full-time operator of Killdozer. I'll get Bucky's company truck, too.

Hours after I should be sleeping, I lay awake and think of Bucky's arrest and how, without the grace of God, Romie could be in jail, too, serving a term a whole lot longer than Bucky will get. Felony offense, selling even a couple of Oxy capsules. Romie sold nearly six hundred.

"You worrying about your friend from work?" Romie turns toward me beneath the covers.

"Yeah."

She somehow reads my mind and lets out a breath that tickles my ear. "What's done is done, Jasper. Ain't no danger in it, now. Nobody's coming for us. We're hundreds of miles and four or five months past that kind of trouble."

I mumble, not sure if I agree with her, or not.

"I know that don't make it right, but it's nothing to worry over now."

"I wasn't worrying about that," I say. "I was thinking about who's gonna do my job, if I'm doing Bucky's."

She knows I'm lying, and her lips find mine before I can tell another untruth.

I hear the screech of the lunch whistle over Killdozer's groan, and I drop the tree I've cleared and shut off the engine right where the forest machine sits. I step down off the dozer and pull on a clean T-shirt, and that's when I hear it—a howling mewl unlike anything I've ever heard. It sends a chill skittering across the back of my neck. I shake off the shudder and stand still, trying to situate the source. It comes again, more of a squeal this time, from the tall stack of broken trees to my right.

My work boots are quiet as I step across the soft ground, lunge over Killdozer's ruts in the rain-damp soil, maneuver around broken knee-high stumps I've yet to tear out. The sweet, pungent scent of fresh pine rosin and maple sap fills the air, and on the breeze, I catch a whiff of the bitter whang of diesel fuel.

The animalistic whimpering grows louder, but when a fallen branch snaps beneath my footfall, it silences. I wonder if I've trapped a cat in the pile of broken trees, except the sound doesn't quite sound like a cat . . . or a squirrel, or a bird, or any small animal I've heard before. Two yards ahead of me, a low blur of movement in a pine bough catches my eye, and I hold my breath as I step alongside the shattered crown of a loblolly pine.

The scrambling movement grows more frantic as I draw near, and again the pained howl erupts, tensing me all over. Small branches crack beneath my boots, and the long fringe of pine needles on the ground in front of me stop moving. I cautiously push them aside, startled to see a smoke-colored rabbit nearly the size of a housecat. The panicked rabbit sees or senses me, lets out a pitiful squeal and furiously digs at the ground in an effort to escape. One of the heavy pine limbs has fallen across the rabbit's hind-parts, pinning it to the ground.

"Shhhh," I whisper. "Be still. I'm here to help you." I squat near the rabbit, reach carefully around its head and grasp the scruff, holding it with one hand while I lift the limb with the other, push it to the side.

The rabbit squeals again, a terrified sound that sends a shiver across my scalp. I hold the creature aloft, and he's badly mangled. He twists in an effort to escape, and his hind legs dangle uselessly, his innards begin to slip loose. I look away, bury my face in my shoulder.

I know what I have to do.

I slide my hands together around the rabbit's warm neck, close my eyes and give a quick twist, hear the soft crunch I feel between my fingers and thumbs. Daddy would call this a mountain-mercy killing. The breeze turns cold. It will soon rain.

I hammer the ground with heel of my boot, carve out a trough where I can bury the rabbit, and that's when I see them. Seven kits. Only two have their eyes open. The limp rabbit I hold was a momma.

I lay her in the trough, and resentment tightens my jaw. I stand, stomp the ground like a temperamental child. Why me? I look at the kits again, each no bigger than my palm. I can't bear wringing their little necks—they're so tiny I'd have to do it with my fingertips. I stare at the momma in the furrow. It would be a slow, cruel death to bury the babies alive with their momma. They have to be killed first.

As I kneel and scoop loose soil over the momma rabbit, I push away the memory of the fistful of dirt I crumbled over Daddy's casket. Fury I can't account for surges through me, and I stand and smack dirt from my hands, look again at the seven kits. Romie's voice speaks in my head—*if we keep on killing the land, the land will have no choice but to kill us right back.*

That works both ways, don't it? Daddy died of Crohn's and cancer caused by the poisoned land. So if the land kills us. . .

I let out a low scream as I stomp my boot-heel into the nest of kits, quickly snuffing their little lives. "You killed my daddy, and you killed Romie's first baby!" I curse the land, tromp at the earth, kick dirt over the rusty, fur-smeared ground, then drag the pine bough to cover my sin. I turn my face to the overcast sky and growl through my teeth like a madman.

I unpocket the key to Killdozer, skip lunch with the guys in the office trailer, stride instead directly back to the machine. No sane man could have an appetite after what I've done.

I brutally attack the trees with Killdozer, grunting and shouting each time I snap one in half. The branches of a tall elm become arms reaching for the sky, and I grasp it in the middle with the grapple, right where I think its heart should be, and I split it in half. It feels good, like the land deserves what I'm doing to it. Soon my rage burns off, and I start to feel sick again. I look behind me at the long row of tree-stacks waiting to be fed to the chipper—more trees than I've ever cleared in an hour—each stack standing higher than Killdozer and me. Tracks and ruts and splintered stumps mark where I've been, and I pause and look around at the woods I've destroyed. Soon, this will all be asphalt.

I drive the dozer between two of the tall stacks, out of sight of the office trailer and the half-dozen men roving the ground in the distance. I climb down and sit on the ground behind the leafy crown of a fallen maple. I hide my face in my knees and try hard not to cry. I cry anyway.

A big empty part of me aches to talk to Daddy one more time, to ask him if what I'm doing is right or wrong. After a few minutes, I climb back onto Killdozer, take a swig of water, and spit it onto the ground. I'm proud of the paycheck I'm earning, of how well I take care of my family, but when I look around me, I'm ashamed. I can't do this much longer.

As I work the last three hours of my shift, my head churns with memories and stories and new ideas, and when I head back to the office trailer to punch out, I've decided it's the last day I'll drive Killdozer. Mack ain't around for me to tell him, so I head home, grateful for the start of cleansing rain, for the heavy traffic that allows me more time to think.

I'll talk to Mack in the morning and tell him I'll take the pay-cut that comes with the step-down. I'll go back to where I started, digging footers again, laying block, building something, instead of tearing things apart. I can't wait to tell Romie.

At the first red traffic light, I remember to turn on my cell phone, in case Romie's called for me to pick up milk or bread or cat food on the way home. Before the traffic even starts moving again, the phone chimes again and again and again with messages, and I know something's wrong. I pull into the first parking lot I come to, hit the speaker button on my cell.

"Jasper, call me as soon as you can." It's Romie.

The next message is also from her. "Something's wrong, Jasper. If I don't hear back from you in ten minutes, I'm going ahead to the hospital."

I let the phone fall into the seat beside me as the third message starts to play, and I punch the gas, cutting into traffic, ignoring the blaring horn from the black Chevy I've nearly sideswiped.

"Jasper, I'm in the E.R. at Women's Hospital. It's the baby." There's a sob in her throat, and I match it with one of my own. "Get here as soon as you can."

I drive too fast, too dangerous, Romie's words sounding again in my head. *If we keep on killing the land. . .* I have done this to her, I think. Part of me knows I haven't caused anything to happen to her or the baby, but another part of me thinks that maybe I have.

There's an empty parking spot in front of the emergency room entrance, and I jump out of the truck and sprint through the hospital's automatic doors. The moon-faced nurse acts as if she's been expecting me, as if she knows who I am, who I'm here to see. I'm surprised when she leads me past the rooms made of green curtains and down a hallway, where she stops beside a private hospital room, holds open the door. She places her hand on my shoulder and looks at me, her eyes sorrowful, and my mouth goes dry.

Inside the dimly lit room, Romie looks small in the hospital bed, and when she looks up at me, she's crying. She holds out a hand, and I take it, sit on the bed beside her, and hold her in my arms while we weep.

The next morning, I help Romie pull on her blouse, wishing I'd thought to go home while she slept to get her a fresh one. The maternity top now hangs in soft folds across her middle. We sit side-by-side on the hospital bed, while we wait for the nurse to complete paperwork and come for us. I stroke Romie's hand.

"I want to go home, Jasper," she says.

"I know, baby. Not long now."

She grips my hand, stops its movement. "Home. Back home. I want to go back to West Virginia."

Back home. Her words strike a familiar ache in me, a throb, like a toothache I've probed with my tongue.

There is no home to return to, no empty house where we began married life together, and the homeplace where I was raised is rented for another year. We sold our trailer and little plot of land to people more rooted than us when we left Stump Branch.

Again, it is as if she pulls thoughts from my head. "I don't want to go back to Stump Branch."

I wonder if this is her way of running, of leaving behind all the bad that has happened. "Where would we go?"

"Morgantown. Maybe Huntington. Shepherdstown." Her shoulder lifts and drops. "A place where there's a good nursing school."

I stare at our hands nestled together, hers smaller than mine, softer, yet somehow much stronger.

Her voice drops to a whisper. "I don't want to do this again, Jasper. No more trying for babies."

She is fraught, upset, grieving. It will pass.

"We don't have to think about that right now. The doctor said to wait six months, get your strength back."

Romie shakes her head, and hair falls over one red-rimmed eye. "No more." Her voice comes stronger, louder. "No more."

I suck in the sadness, the hopelessness in her voice, swallow it down where it tightens like a fist, hard and cold in my stomach. "Okay. No more."

Daddy once told me the greatest joy of a man's life was a walk through the woods with his child. There will be no child for me. *No woods, either.* No coal mining. No slaying trees. No babies. No more. My scalp prickles.

I try to imagine what the future holds, where Romie and I will live—just the two of us, no child to bring us joy in old age. Where will I work? What will I do with the rest of my days? I close my eyes, but I can't picture anything at all, can't see what lies ahead, only blackness like I found in the belly of the earth. There's a void there, a nothingness, a big empty so powerful I still taste its icy bitterness in my mouth.

A Word—and a World—of Thanks

To Press 53: Kevin Watson, publisher, for believing in me, and Claire V. Foxx, editor, for your eagle eyes.

To the Critical Critique Crew: Cheryl Russell, Doreen Leone, Matthew McEver, Kristina Cooper Atkins, Kevin Welch, Gabrielle Brant Freeman, Kristi Hebert, Travis Burnham, Phillip Morris, Sonja Condit, Clay Snellgrove, Karin Gillespie, Jenn and Jeremi Mondello, Graham Norse, Mark Vickers, Rosa Sophia, Pamela Akins, Luis Castillo, Bob Dolan, David Allan Kelly, Margaret Kirby, Michelle K. Nelson, Leigh Raper, and Sandy Tritt. This is your success as much as it is mine.

To the Cheerleaders and Early Readers: Jacob White, Becky Gray, Joe and Robin Fenwick, Ron and Paula Johnson, Paul "Snap" Kinner, Morgan White, Bethany DiMaggio, David Lifsey, Pam Hanson, Kathy Kish, and The Roost Crew.

To the Masterful Mentors: Les Standiford, Stewart O'Nan, Leslie Pietrzyk, Marlin Barton, Robert M. Olmstead, Edward Falco, and Keith Lee Morris.

To Those Who Pushed Me Up the Mountain: Momma and Daddy (a.k.a. Willis and Nilene Browning), Robert W. Walker, Rachel Bragg, Benjamin Campbell, Vanessa Thompson, Chris Kuell, Rick Mulkey, Susan Tekulve, Richard Tillinghast, Kirk Judd, Wilma Acree, Patsy Pittman, Charlotte Firbank King, Wendy Chorot, Sandi Rog, Jimmy Carl Harris, Geoff Fuller, West Virginia Writers, Inc., The Inkslingers, Converse College Low-Residency MFA Program, and Eckerd College Writers in Paradise.

In Memorium: Heartfelt gratitude is owed to my precious mother-in-law, Georgia Etter White, who was always pleasantly surprised when I created anything of substance. Special thanks to my late and sorely missed friend and critique partner, Terry W. McNemar. I know you're proud of this li'l girl, bubba.

Rhonda Browning White resides near Daytona Beach, Florida. Her work appears in *Qu Literary Journal*, *Hospital Drive*, *HeartWood Literary Review*, *Bellevue Literary Review*, *Steel Toe Review*, *Ploughshares Writing Lessons*, *Tiny Text*, *NewPages*, *South 85 Journal*, *The Skinny Poetry Journal*, *WV Executive*, *Mountain Echoes*, *Gambit*, *Justus Roux*, *Bluestone Review*, and in the anthologies *Ice Cream Secrets*, *Appalachia's Last Stand*, and *Mountain Voices*. She holds an MFA in Creative Writing from Converse College in Spartanburg, South Carolina, and has been awarded a fellowship from Eckerd College's Writers in Paradise. *The Lightness of Water & Other Stories* is her debut story collection. She is working on a novel.

CPSIA information can be obtained
at www.ICGtesting.com
Printed in the USA
BVHW072320180919
558851BV00001B/6/P